WITCHCRAFT IN THE HAREM

STORIES BY
ALIYA WHITELEY

First edition published by
Dog Horn Publishing
45 Monk Ings, Birstall, Batley WF17 9HU
United Kingdom
doghornpublishing.com

ISBN 978-1-907133-40-4

Cover design by
Adam Lowe

Typesetting by
Jonathan Penton

Sales Representation: Richard Boundy
richard:doghornpublishing

UK Distribution: Central Books
99 Wallis Road, London, E9 5LN, United Kingdom
orders@centralbooks.com
Phone:+44 (0) 845 458 9911
Fax: +44 (0) 845 458 9912

Overseas Distribution: Printondemand-worldwide.com
9 Culley Court, Orton Southgate, Peterborough, PE2 6XD,
United Kingdom
info@printondemand-worldwide.com
Phone: +44 (0) 1733 237 867
Fax: +44 (0)1733 234 309

WITCHCRAFT IN THE HAREM

For Elsa

TABLE OF CONTENTS

GALATEA

Leon was a lonely orphan, and he loved to look at flesh.

After leaving school at sixteen with an appreciation of classical sculpture and no interest in a real career, he took a job as a receptionist in a naturist resort so he could watch the bending and twisting of skin during volleyball, the bunching of muscles as ping-pong was played, the diamond patterns of fat on the buttocks of sunbathers.

But really he wanted to put aside his binoculars and leave his receptionist's hut behind; he wanted to touch. He saw no reason why he shouldn't, but the naturists complained when he sneaked up behind them, his hands splayed and ready to grab, and the job was taken away.

He signed up for benefits and got a flat in a city. Then there was only one answer to his need for flesh.

Clay.

He bought pounds of it, and took it back to the living room of his tiny flat.

Smooth between the fingers, it seemed to make itself into the shape of a woman, and it was easy to form the breasts to his palms and then pinch the nipples into being. His years of devotion to flesh flowed through his hands and into his creation, and when he was finished, she was quite, quite perfect.

'Galatea,' he whispered against her cold lips.

That night, for the first and last time, he prayed. And in the morning, he opened his eyes and saw her in the corner of his bedroom. She had walked there. She was watching him.

'Galatea,' he breathed. He got out of bed. He touched her arm.

She's warm… if this be magic, let it be an art lawful as eating…

He kissed her. She kissed him back, but she would not open her lips. He examined her nostrils, and between her legs: there were no holes in her. She was solid.

9

But she was flesh, and he loved her. He told her to exercise, then stroked her as she stretched, and touched the twists in her torso. He slapped her buttocks and watched the ripples. He licked his finger and ran it from her pert nose to her perfect navel.

For one week, it was enough.

But one week and one day passed, and he discovered he wanted more. He wanted to penetrate.

He told her to lie on his bed. Then he took a pair of scissors, and tried to cut apart her lips. The blades slipped into her flesh, but when he pulled them out, the cut he had made closed without a seam.

So he took a skewer, and held it over the flame of his two ring gas hob until it was white hot. Then he told her to open her legs, and he thrust the skewer between them, up into her, so that the tip of the skewer must have reached to that perfect navel. He left it there to cool.

But when he came back, hours later, he found there was nothing to pull free. The skewer had vanished. Her flesh had simply sucked it in and closed around it.

So he took his garden shears and snipped off one finger at a time, looking for a hole, or just one air bubble, anything to show that she could be hollowed out.

Nothing.

Then he took off her toes.

Nothing.

Then he took his largest kitchen knife and sliced her, thinly, from her toe stumps upwards, through her knees, thighs, hips, ribs and shoulders. And finally, a miniscule amount of flesh at a time, he cut through her face until he reached the very top of her head.

Nothing.

'Galatea,' he said.

But on the bed there was only a scattering of wafer-thin pink shreds, like the feathers of a flamingo that had flown away.

WITCHCRAFT IN THE HAREM

On the plane, drinking a quarter-bottle of white, I retrieved my address book from my crocodile bag, tore out a page at a time, and turned each one into a snowflake with a few painless tears. The man sitting next to me, tall with a clean suit and pale skin, brushed away the white shreds that fell on his lap with the back of his hand. I resolved to be more like him. He didn't look anywhere but straight ahead.

'I'm Bobbie,' I said. And then I thought about the Stuff.

The Stuff was gone. Destroyed. There was no place on Earth where Becky and The Designer would not find me.

Last time I saw Becky, she was on the catwalk, left breast bared and painted yellow, skirt of razor blades clacking against her thighs. She gave her three-quarter turn and clocked me in the back row. Her eyes took in my newly shorn hair, but I couldn't tell what she thought of it from her somnambulistic stare. Then she flicked back up the catwalk and was gone.

Two hours later I had boarded this flight.

'I'm in serious trouble here,' I said to the pale man. 'Give me some words of wisdom.'

He didn't say anything. Not too surprising, considering he was being confronted by a six feet two ex-model in a red micro-mini and a see-through blouse.

'Cat got your tongue?' I asked.

He tilted his head towards me and opened his mouth, so wide that at first I thought he was going to attempt to swallow me. But he stayed like that, and behind the yellowing row of his bottom teeth was a writhing stump, like a blind worm in the darkness: all that remained of a tongue.

11

I had nothing and nowhere, and I needed to plant a seed. I put my hand on the back of his neck and pulled him towards me so I could kiss his open mouth; those pale soft lips were as refreshing as water on my foundation-caked face. 'Take me home with you,' I said. Perhaps he didn't understand, but he made no comment when the plane landed and I followed him through the airport. I boarded the small black jet that waited for him and smiled at him during the seven hour flight to destination safe haven.

The plane landed on a white runway that was the only strip of land jutting out into a large blue-green bay. I had found no place on Earth. Even I didn't know where I was.

He had a harem, of course. I was the first white woman. Nobody spoke my language, but that was fine; I've never really got on with women anyway, not even Becky. You would think being twin sisters would be enough to form a bond, but she was raised with my mother and I went to my father after the divorce. We didn't meet again for years, and when I tracked her down in Paris she introduced me to the Designer and the Stuff, and asked me to live with them. I suppose she liked the novelty of having a double: every man's fantasy, so they say. So sharing a man was not a new thing for me, and I was comfortable in the communal room, even if I ignored the women and they ignored me.

I would have liked a fountain, though. I've seen films with scenes in harems and there were always fountains in the centre of the room. Our room was more like a large lounge: lots of sofas, comfortable chairs and cushions, and a tiny kitchenette hidden behind a glass brick wall, with a microwave and a coffee machine. Food was always provided, but occasionally the girls would make strong, syrupy coffee which couldn't have done them any good. I stuck to water.

The bell was the summons to the man with no tongue. It was a brass circle with a clapper attached by a small rod, fixed above the only door. It reminded me of the bell above the blackboard that I used to watch during those long, boring afternoons in the classroom, the teacher droning on and the other pupils flicking pencils at my head; I've never been popular in group situations.

12

There was a code to the rings, and every woman knew it. The others had demonstrated my call sign to me upon my arrival; I was three long and two short. It rang for me perhaps twice a week. I think I was too vocal for him. It was a Western habit I couldn't shake off.

There were windows, but not much of a view. The ocean stretched away to nothing. The sky was always cloudless. Sometimes I wondered if we were on a huge boat, but I felt no movement. Maybe it was a tiny island, uncharted, hidden like a sequin that nestles in the ruffled bodice of an emerald silk dress; a place of secrecy and beauty.

A place where laws did not exist. A place where magic and murder could bleed together.

The flavour of the month was Fasheema. She had wedding-dress white hair and was maybe five feet tall on tiptoe. All the women walked everywhere on tiptoe, their arms swinging backwards and forwards in graceful movements timed precisely to match their steps, trying so hard to look as if relaxation came naturally to them. It was always a competition, and Fasheema was winning it hands down. Every day, at about midday I would guess by the position of the sun through the window, she was summoned by the man with no tongue with two short rings of the bell. She would make her way out of the harem with the languid swaying of an anemone in an undisturbed rock pool; she knew she was invincible.

Putting all those women together in one place was asking for trouble.

I knew what the looks meant, and I wasn't surprised when they gathered in the kitchen one day after Fasheema had gone forth to do her duty. I was ignored, of course, but that made it easy to watch them from my position in the far corner amongst a nest of silk cushions.

Some lifted their long skirts and from under them produced twisted papers that contained pinches of bright powder, or spindly black roots. Others slid delicate orange and yellow flowers from between their breasts, cupping their hands under the petals as if

13

they had drawn out their hearts for inspection. One woman with enormous hips opened her mouth and extended her tongue to allow the iridescent purple beetle upon it to be captured. It was then squashed into a smear and added to the white china bowl was used to hold the precious possessions.

The women stroked the bowl, one at a time, as it was passed between them. They cradled it and caressed it, and their movements lulled me towards sleep. I reclined on the fluffy cushions and only kept my eyes open for long enough to see them place the bowl in the microwave and set it turning on that little glass disc for a total of five of your Earth minutes.

That's something the Designer used to say. *Just five of your Earth minutes, Bobbie and Becky, to try on this teaspoon hat and this Rizla blouse,* and we would come down from our private cloud to let ourselves be adorned with his creations. Then, as a reward, he would give us a taste of Stuff from the drawer in his Victorian mahogany cabinet, unlocking it with that key he always kept on a ruby encrusted chain around his neck.

I never thought he'd sleep deeply enough for me to be able to take that chain from him. But it turns out that we all fall into unwakeable sleep sometimes, just as I did on those silk cushions that afternoon. I had an intense vision, filled with grass that tickled my feet, and beetles that crawled across my face, and Becky was there, groaning in rapture, carpeted in black roots that grew over her statuesque body and into her hair. She looked as natural as a tree.

When I came around no time at all could have passed. The microwave door was open and the women were sitting on the floor in a circle a few feet away, their long skirts arranged behind them like the petals of some enormous carnivorous flower.

The china bowl was in the centre of their circle. Inside it was a mustard yellow powder, flecked with tiny green crystals. I never thought I'd see that powder again.

'Stuff!' I said.

The women raised their heads as one and stared at me. The one with the large hips flicked her hands in what I took to be a gesture of warning.

'Is this where all the Stuff gets made, then?' I asked. 'Do you make all the Stuff in the world? Is that why the man with no tongue is so rich? Who comes here to pick it up? Is it the Designer?' But, of course, they didn't understand me and I couldn't have understood their replies if they had deigned to give one.

It seemed this wasn't the last place on Earth after all.

They crowded closer together, closing in on themselves, and I could no longer see the bowl. There was nothing I could do but lie back once more. Only a few minutes later Fasheema returned from her daily appointment, swinging her arms to her private internal melody. She looked as smug as ever.

I knew what was going to happen as soon as they brought that cup of coffee to her.

They passed it to her on a silver tray, and she accepted it with an incline of her head, as if they had finally noticed how superior she was and it was her right to be served in such a manner.

It took only one swallow to do its job.

As I watched her go through the transformation that comes from overdose, I felt the pull of the Stuff upon me. I wondered how I could ever have found the willpower to destroy it, and try to escape it. As Fasheema went through the soundless alteration which leads to death, I could see the absolute ecstasy of freedom on her face, and I wanted to feel it too, even if it meant the cracking of my bones and the contortion of my skin.

By the time her heart gave out she was unrecognisable. Patches of fur vied with protruding growths of reptile skin, and around what had once been her neck was a ruff of soft pink feathers. There weren't arms and legs anymore; instead there were yellowed spidering roots. Her body looked like a tuber that had just been dug up and left on the floor for weeks. The only thing that was unchanged was her hair; startling white against the mess that she had become, it splayed out on the floor like a skein of silk that had been thrown away.

The women cut the hair and stuffed it into one of the silk cushions. They diced the remains of Fasheema and threw her out of the window into the waiting sea, to be taken away by the tide. They did it quickly and with no fuss as if they had done it before.

15

The next day, the bell went for Fasheema. Nobody moved, or even glanced at the bell. They sat as still as sculptures, practising their attitudes of blamelessness until the man with no tongue arrived and looked over them with a blank expression. He didn't seem to really see them at all, so they stopped posturing and went back to their quiet conversations in their strange language.

'Hard luck, Buster,' I said. 'She's gone. Out of the window. Away on the tide.'

Everyone stared at me. I'd be lying if I didn't admit it was nice to be the centre of attention again, if only for a moment. I've always been the woman everyone looks twice at, right from when I first sprouted breasts and legs of magnifique proportions. I'm not saying it won me many friends, but it did make me special. I hadn't realised how much I missed that.

The man with no tongue smiled. Then he made a gesture that I understood. He raised one hand, extended his index finger, and waggled it back and forth. *You're a naughty minx, but I like you.*

The waggle changed to a beckon, and I followed him out of the harem.

After that the bell rang three long and two short every day, and I knew I was in trouble.

It took the women three weeks of my summonings to decide they'd had enough. I returned from the man with no tongue late one afternoon, the red sunlight just crawling through the bottom corner of the window, to find them gathered in their circle, eyes cast down as if in pious contemplation. In the centre of the gathering was the silver tray, and placed upon that was one cup of syrupy black coffee.

I stepped into the circle, knelt down, and took the cup in both hands. The warmth of the coffee was soothing. I looked into the faces of the women surrounding me and felt the chill of their stares chase away that comfort.

'Bobbie?'

The last hint of daylight faded. I turned my head to the window and locked eyes with two shadows.

16

'We found you,' Becky said. Her hair was loose and her smile was real. She was wearing a necklace of razor blades that had the Designer's touch about it, for sure. I'd never seen her look so happy.

'Isn't she beautiful?' the Designer said. 'So beautiful it hurts.' He craned his neck to see further into the room. 'You could be this beautiful if you're prepared to give up this dump and come with us.'

'I am so bloody sorry,' I said. 'About the Stuff. About everything.'

He shrugged. 'We got more. It set us free. Free to that place inside us. Now we're staying forever. Will you come too?'

I thought about it. There really didn't seem to be anything worth staying for; not the man who would never speak to me, or the women who wanted me gone.

'Okay,' I said. I picked up the coffee cup, drained it, and floated out through the window.

And now I really have found no place on Earth.

There are others floating nearby; I think I saw Fasheema once, curled up in a pink cloud like a well-fed cat in a padded basket. But we do not talk to the others. We don't need them. We are together.

We three who sleep amongst the stars and swim in the eternal sea. My twin, the Designer, and me.

WINGSPAN

When the mass insanity struck life went on as normal.

It was different in everyone, and some people got it worse than others, but generally it was just a feeling that things were not the way we thought they were. So if you looked at your husband and his head had turned into an aubergine, you knew that it was the insanity – coined 'the dribbles' by the newspapers – and you could ignore it until it went away again.

I got it bad. And Terry's head hasn't yet stopped being an aubergine, and the cat is still singing the *Queen of the Night* aria from *The Magic Flute* on the back fence at night, and the cutlery still cowers away and hisses at me when I open the kitchen drawer. I try not to think about it. I watch Terry's giant purple head split open to reveal a soft white pulp mouth as he tells me he still loves me, even if I can't bring myself to kiss him anymore. There's something lofty in his tone; perhaps he thinks he's better than me. After all, he got over the delusion that I was Blackpool Pleasure Beach in a matter of days. He must be stronger in his mind, somehow, mustn't he?

This morning, as he sleeps, I notice a bruise on one side of his head. The purple flesh is turning yellow. I'm hoping it doesn't start to go mouldy. I think that might be the nail in the coffin of our relationship.

*

I work as a cleaner in a large insurance office in the centre of town. I work alone.

I used to be a social worker, but the dribbles put an end to that. The social order has changed, you see. When I pass the tramps and drug addicts in doorways as I scuttle along in the early hours to get to work, I know they have the disease worse than me. If I happen to see a smartly dressed commuter, I know they hardly have it at all. The dribbling underclass is not made up solely of people who never had a good start, never went to university, never had the right colour skin. The shivering wreck, the one with the patchy beard and the bloodshot eyes, who lies on the steps of the Natwest and always shouts 'Fore!' at me as I hurry past – he used to be the manager there. He granted Terry and me our first mortgage. I always find myself wondering if he used to be fond of golf. What does he see when he looks at me? Am I a buggy or a club? A diamond patterned sweater or a little white ball?

*

The spring sun has just made it over the top of the buildings when I see the running man emerging from the alley ahead. He has the legs of a flamingo and he moves without grace, those pink sticks with knobbly knees bending and straightening. From behind him comes a pterodactyl with a small black gun held in one front paw. The pterodactyl bellows, a tremendous noise like metal grinding on metal, and the flamingo man keeps running. As he gets nearer I can hear him panting, 'no, no' in time with his quick breaths. He's only a few steps away from me when the gun fires.

It's a real sound. I really hear the eardrum-popping sound of a fired gun. I clap my hands over my ears and flamingo man drops to his knees in front of me, and the reality of it is thick, and strong, and horrible. Then the flowers start to pour from his body, fluttering on to the road, red rose petals everywhere – so many petals come from him, it's incredible, and the sweet smell is intense, cloying.

There's the sound of sirens, getting closer.

The pterodactyl turns in the direction of the sirens, and then looks at me. His reptilian yellow eyes weigh up the possibilities. He squeezes his leathery body back into the alley. I watch until his tail disappears.

Flamingo man, still on his knees, flails with his arms. He catches my elbow, pulls me down to him. 'Pocket,' he says. He falls to the side, away from me, and his head hits the road. I hear a noise

19

like a knife plunging into a melon. Is that a real sound or not? He sighs, a long, long, sigh that ends in a chuckle. The sirens are very loud now. I reach into his suit pocket, the one nearest to me, and find a small white cardboard box.

'No,' he says.

I take the box and get back to my feet, moving out of the range of his twitching bird legs. They bang against the ground, jerking, fitting. The police cars come into view – the flashing sirens are bouncing beach balls. I wait for them to arrive.

*

In the solitude of the office, standing by the windows, all the computers smacking their lips together and all the chairs performing star-jumps, I take out the white cardboard box and stare at it.

I didn't tell the police. I put this down in part to the four officers present being grandfather clocks with annoyingly monotonous ticks, and in part to my own stupidity. I am really idiotic to get involved with this, even if the box is an adventure I've been longing for, even if flamingo man did look at me as if I was meant to have it.

I open the box.

Inside is a blister pack of pills, thirty in total, small and pink under the shiny blue foil. And below the pack is a piece of paper with tiny printed words upon it. I have to hold it close to my eyes to read it.

WARNING: EXPERIMENTAL
ONE A DAY, TO BE TAKEN WITH A FULL GLASS OF WATER
24HR MONITORING OF PATIENT RECOMMENDED

I turned over the paper. In red pen, in a rushed messy hand, were the words:

Bernie – leave the money with Mike,
take the stuff and kiss your dribbles goodbye!
Glad we could help. Tom.

20

I'm not stupid. I'm just insane. And I know what I'm holding in my hands. I pop the first one from the packet and swallow it down before it turns into a frog and hops away. I pocket the blister pack and the card, throw away the box, and skirt the jumping chairs to get to the water cooler, which is currently masquerading as a pottery vase.

I wonder many things as I clean: how long it will take to start working; what the side-effects will be; how I could have been so lucky; how much money this secret drug trades for; and where this apparent cure could have originated from. It doesn't surprise me that flamingo man was killed over it. The only thing that surprises me is how little I care about what might happen to me. I never knew how much I hated the dribbles until I discovered that I didn't have to put up with it for the rest of my life.

I clean and I wait. I clean, and I wait.

*

I preferred Terry with the head of an aubergine.

Not that I've told him about the pills. The pills are a secret. I've taken twenty of them so far. Ten days to go, and then I have no idea what might happen to me. Will the dribbles return or redouble? Will some horrible mental anguish afflict me? Or will I be cured forever?

I'm beginning to think 'cured' is a relative term.

'That was great,' says Terry. He rolls off me, puts his face close to mine on the pillow, our noses nearly touching. I can see blackheads lurking in the folds of his skin, the places he misses when he washes. He has grey nasal hair sprouting in clumps, the ends blunt from previous attempts to trim it, and greenish gunk in the corners of his eyes that look as if it hasn't been disturbed for weeks.

'Yes, brilliant,' I say.

'I'm so glad you're cured. I knew you'd get over it eventually. I had faith in you.'

'Thanks,' I say. 'I really need a wee.'

I get up, put on my very boring brown dressing gown, which is no longer a gorilla costume, and lock the door to the en-suite behind me. I sit on the toilet for a while, then run some clear water from the tap-shaped tap, and clean my teeth with the toothbrush-shaped toothbrush.

I think of smooth-skinned aubergines, that luscious purple flesh and how easy it is to tell when one is rotten, going bad, the mould spreading a little further every day.

The doorbell makes a doorbell noise.

'What time is it?' calls Terry in his annoyed voice.

'Past eleven,' I call back.

The doorbell does its predictable thing again. 'I'll go,' I call. 'You stay put.' It's a good excuse not to look at him as I hurry out of the toilet and down the perfectly regular stairs.

*

I don't recognise his face, but I recognise the small black gun.

'Give them to me,' he says.

'What?'

'Don't play dumb with me. Give me the pills. I need the pills.' He's got big shoulders under that sweaty tee shirt, and his nostrils are flared wide. He holds the gun very still, pointed at my chest, but his eyes move constantly over my face, from my forehead to my nose to my mouth and back to my forehead again. I don't feel fear. I feel pity for this ex-pterodactyl.

'You've got it really bad?'

'What?' he says. 'No.'

'The dribbles.'

'Just give me the pills!'

'I've taken most of them.' He groans. 'I'm sorry! But I have it too... had it. Really bad. I mean really bad. My husband's head was an aubergine for years.'

His hand tightens around the gun, and then he drops it to his side. 'Oh God. I'm so desperate. I can't afford to buy more pills. I only found out about them by accident. My boss was talking to some model he's been dating, and they were saying… they were saying….'

I put my hand out to him, on his broad shoulder. He lets out a loud sob. 'I killed that man for nothing. He was a dealer. I found him, begged him to take everything, my house, my car, but he laughed in my face, said it was nowhere near enough. So I killed him.'

'Why didn't you kill me too?'

He shakes his head and his eyes rest on mine. He smiles, a tiny upturn of his sad mouth. 'I couldn't,' he whispers. 'You're the most beautiful pterodactyl I've ever seen.'

It's the best compliment of my life. 'Take the pills,' I tell him. 'I'll fetch them now.'

'It's no good. It only works if you take the whole course. Then you're cured. If you take less than the full amount, the effect is only temporary.'

I hear Terry shuffling about at the top of the stairs. 'Who is it?'

'Bye,' says the ex-pterodactyl. 'Thanks for listening. Have a good life.' He presses a kiss on my cheek and runs away, into the night.

*

I need to know the reality of the situation. The truth.

It's two days since I've thrown the rest of the pills away, and I look up from my dinner, over the cruet set, to find Terry's head is, once more, an aubergine.

It's more than that. It's a rotten aubergine, the skin split and yellowed, the puffy flesh turning black and the pulp oozing over the collar of his shirt. The smell is disgusting. I can't finish dinner, but that's okay, because my pork chop has turned into a spatula and my mashed potatoes are ladybirds, a pile of them, lying on their backs, black legs wiggling, wriggling, moving fast and getting nowhere.

So that's the reality. The truth.

I push back my chair and clear my throat. 'Terry,' I say. 'This marriage is over. Goodbye. Thanks for everything.'

The aubergine splits apart and grey chunks run down the front of his shirt as he says, 'Why? Hang on! Talk to me! Where are you going?'

'To find a pterodactyl,' I tell him. Then I'm out of the house and running down the yellow brick road, and the trees are singing a medley from *My Fair Lady*, and the stars are dollops of ice cream dripping their sweetness on to my head, blessing me with endless sugar, and I'm grateful, so grateful, I sprout wings and fly.

BABYHEAD

Cynthia couldn't explain what she'd just seen in the vegetable patch. She didn't want to look again. She considered going back into the house, crawling back into bed with Mikey, and putting it down as a beer-inspired dream. But that pinkish dome with the fuzzy down had felt soft under her fingers, and there had been the smell of manufactured newness, like a dusting of talcum powder wafting up to her nostrils, as she had pulled the coarse outer leaves of the cabbage apart.

And there had definitely been a face, scrunched-up, tiny eyes shut tight, mouth folded in on itself like a bud.

She put her gardening gloves back on, crouched down, and looked at the top of the cabbage again.

The baby's head was still there.

It nestled between the thick, caterpillar-munched leaves that had begun to peel back in the sun. She could see the curve of the skull, the two delicate ears, even the soft spot on the top – the fontanelle. The word came to her from holding her sister's baby, little Rosalie, years ago, and her sister's warning about the bones not yet having fused together. Pulling back the leaves further to see the face clearly, it struck Cyn that this baby looked very much like Rosalie had back then. Or perhaps all babies looked alike. Except, she reminded herself, this wasn't a baby. She patted the earth around the base of the cabbage. It was moist from the rain the night before, and packed tight. Nobody had touched it.

A cat meowed, close by, a thin sound. Cyn jerked up her head and scanned the garden, trying to pinpoint it. After a moment she realised it was coming from the head. The little mouth opened and closed; a purple tongue emerged and quivered as the head cried.

Cyn ran back to the house. She took the stairs two at a time, and flung open the door of her darkened bedroom. It smelled of beer and sweat. Mikey was a lump in the crumpled duvet, with nothing visible but the thick brown hair on the top of his head, forming a clumped wedge from the gel that had yet to be washed away. She sat next to him and pulled back the duvet. He screwed up his eyes and curled into a tight ball. 'Ten more minutes.'

'There's a thing in my cabbages.'

He coughed. 'What, like a slug?'

'No. I can't explain it. Come and see.'

'What?'

'It's a head. You have to get up.'

He opened his eyes and frowned at her; maybe he hadn't heard her correctly. 'In a minute –'

'Now.' She pushed the duvet on to the floor, and he grumbled and flailed his skinny white limbs before admitting defeat. Cyn watched him shrug on his tee shirt and jeans from the night before, feeling a mixture of annoyance and gratitude. Ending up in bed with him again had not been part of her plan for the evening, but at least it meant somebody else was around to help her decide what to do. She couldn't begin to imagine how she would have dealt with it alone.

She followed him down the stairs and then took the lead across the lawn, past the roses she so carefully maintained and the clematis that climbed the supports of her swing seat. Dread permeated the quiet joy of her private space, her sanctuary, as Mikey stomped along behind her and she approached the vegetable patch once more. She stopped at the edge of the grass, where the straight lines of the soil began, and pointed into the cabbages.

'There.'

'Which one?'

'The fourth in from the left, on the second row. No, the right, fourth in from the right.'

'Just show me,' he said, in tone which made her certain that breaking up with him would be the right thing to do, if only she could get round to it. She shuffled forward, as close as she dared to stand, and caught a glimpse of the peachy head through the veined leaves. She put one hand to her mouth and pointed more vigorously with the other.

'Right.' He bent down and roughly pulled apart the outside of the cabbage. Then he stopped, suddenly, and she heard his breathing, hard, over the hum of the main road past the fields beyond her fence.

At least the baby had stopped crying.

Not a baby, she reminded herself, as Mikey took his fingers slowly away from the cabbage. 'Jesus,' he said. He turned his head to one side and spat, a fat white glob that landed in the soil. She fought down the urge to be sick.

'It's not... alive, is it?' she said.

'It's moving its mouth.'

'It was crying, earlier.'

He patted the earth around the base of the cabbage, just as she had done, pressing his hands into the soil. 'It's not been touched.'

'No. Should we call someone?'

'It must be buried in the...' He slipped his fingers around the bottom of the leaves and gave a quick tug.

'I don't think you should...' she said, but he grasped it firmly and put effort into his tugging, until she heard the roots begin to give, and saw the soil lift, just a little; the cracked whining of the head started up once more, pitiful, painful to hear.

'Stop!' She hit his shoulder-blades with the flat of her hands until he sat back on his haunches and looked up at her, his eyebrows raised. She pushed past him and knelt down to look into the baby's face. The eyes were open, a clouded blue, and its puckered lips were filmy with blood. It cried and coughed, and a trickle of blood ran from its mouth, over its chin. 'You've hurt it. Call someone!'

'Like who?'

'I don't know, an ambulance...' she said, but he didn't move, and neither did she. The coughing got worse, and turned to gasping; the face changed colour as she watched, to a bluish-

27

white, and then it stopped trying to breathe at all, the eyes rolled backwards and the tongue, now turning black, protruded from the bloody mouth at an awkward, unnatural angle.

Mikey bent down and snatched up the cabbage, flinging earth into the air as he wrenched it free, then tucked it under his arm and marched away from the house, to the fence at the end of the garden. Cyn watched him go, saw him throw it, hard, into the rough ground that formed a barrier between her house and the field that the farmer used for sugar beets. Then he came back, stopped in front of her, and looked at her forehead, not meeting her eyes. 'Right,' he said.

'What did you do?'

'Dealt with it.'

'But what if –'

'I don't know, all right?' he said. 'Animals will eat it. It'll be gone in a few hours. There are loads of things around here that will clear it up. I've got to get going.'

'Where?' she asked his back as he walked away.

Then she remembered that she didn't care anymore. She thought about going to the fence, looking over it, but instead pushed earth into the hole left by the uprooted cabbage with her toe, and pressed it down with her foot until it looked like nothing had ever grown there at all.

*

When she got into bed that night it still smelled of Mikey. She wished she'd remembered to change the sheets and air the room, but hadn't got further than lying on the sofa, watching whatever came on the television that required no thought, after he left.

Cyn flipped over the pillow and hit it with the flat of her hand, then lay back and tried to find sleep.

It wouldn't come.

Out in the dark, she heard singing.

She got up, walked over to the window, and twitched back the curtain just a little, to give her a view of the garden and beyond. Nothing moved. It was a still night, the sky a dark blue with faint streaks of purple remaining from the late sunset. In the distance, the trees rose up together, and the farmer's field stretched out in patterned ridges. The garden was no different than usual. The swing seat did not move. The clematis and the roses sat dormant, waiting for the morning. The runner beans curled around their poles and the cabbages squatted in the earth, drawing nourishment into their thick, veined leaves.

It was singing. Somewhere out there, where she couldn't see it, it was singing strange words, baby words between sense and nonsense, in the darkness, alive and bleeding into the soil.

She dropped the curtain, ran down the stairs, through the kitchen, out into the warm night. The cold grass tickled her bare feet. At the bottom of the garden she climbed over the fence, caught the hem of her nightdress on a nail, fell, and scrambled on her hands and knees to the edge of the field. The singing faded, petered away into silence.

Above, the ribbons of faint light remained for a few moments, like the pattern of a worn blanket. Underneath it babies were being put to bed, so many babies, soft in body and cosseted in mother love; they were being deposited in high-sided cots, their blankets warm, their foreheads kissed, their mobiles spinning onwards, onwards in their circles.

She searched the field until it was too dark to see her hands moving over the soil. There was nothing. The baby did not sing again.

*

Cyn stepped into the bar and scanned it until she spotted him, at one of the back tables, straddling the bench seat with one pint in his hands and another lined up in front of him. He was with the usual group from his office; they were laughing at something. She could tell from the way his shoulders moved that he was laughing too, even though his back was to her.

The music was too loud, and the room too crowded for her. She'd phoned in sick, spent all week at home, listening out for only one sound. To be surrounded by voices was nearly too much for her, but Cyn fought down her panic and wound her way through the crowds to stand behind him.

She tapped him on the shoulder, and when he turned around to look up at her, his smile fell away.

'I need your help,' she said.

'Oh yeah?'

'I can't sleep. It keeps making noises.'

'What does?'

At first she wasn't sure she'd heard him correctly. But from the way he was looking at her, with hostile eyes, his chin set, she began to understand the situation.

'You know what,' she said.

'No, I don't.'

'You getting a round in, Cyn?' said one of his friends: Graham, the tall one.

'No,' she told him.

'If you're not drinking, there's no point in being here,' said Mikey, with a smirk to his friend, who pulled amused, complicit faces back.

She crouched down in front of him and put her mouth up close to his ear. He had always had nice ears, small for a man, with soft flesh and delicate lobes. 'Please don't do this,' she whispered. 'It's still alive. I need you to help me find it. I've spent nights out there.'

He turned his face into hers so he could whisper back, 'You know what you should do?'

'What?'

'Move house.'

He sat back, away from her, and Cyn stood up and walked away, pushing back through the laughter and the shouting and the spilling of beer. Outside the pub, she waited for a while, in the warm yellow light from the doorway of the fish and chip shop opposite, but Mikey didn't come out. If he had, she didn't know what she would have said anyway.

*

She spent all her time outside, in the tent she'd put up by the vegetable patch. The singing came and went; she'd stopped trying to find it. Instead she listened, and sometimes shouted out how sorry she was over the field. And she watched the cabbages with their roots still deep in the soil.

Inside her, there was the sense of waiting. Of growing without seeing, of becoming without knowing. An event was coming. Something momentous. She expected to be changed in ways she couldn't imagine, and so she didn't try to imagine it. She let it come to her, in small crawlings, inching out of her.

It happened at the end of summer.

She hadn't been to work in months and they'd stopped paying her. It didn't matter, not when she woke up, crawled out of her tent, and saw those dusky pink curves emerge from the leaves and open their eyes for her.

Cyn counted them. Seven. Seven little baby heads, all perfect, all nestled in the cabbages, little mouths, little tongues, tiny little noses. It was impossible to tell them apart, but she supposed it would come to her in time, the differences that made them unique.

'Darlings,' she said.

She knelt down amongst them and stroked their heads, their eyes, their peachy cheeks. Her body responded to the soft smell of them; she felt her womb and her heart expanding with love.

The voice reached her from the field. It sang strange words, clear in the dawn, and the blind blue eyes of the new ones turned in its direction as one. The singing grew louder. She stood up, climbed over the back fence, and followed it to the field.

31

This time she found the head. In the rows of sugar beets, buried under a seething mass of worms and flies, with its eyes eaten and the sockets sunken with maggots, with a ragged, writhing hole where its lips and tongue should be, still it sang on. Cyn picked it up, brushed off as many of the insects as she could, and carried it back to the others. She sat cross-legged in the middle of the cabbage patch, and held it in her lap, against her abdomen, stroking it, hoping it knew how much she wanted it.

The dawn turned into daylight, clear and hot and strong, and they looked at her with such trusting expectation.

Cyn lay down in the dirt and let their love impregnate her.

1926 IN BRAZILIAN FOOTBALL

Thursday

This is not going to be a story about football.

This is a story about frogs.

I saw my first frog at the age of five. I was in Mrs Clark's class, and our spring visit to the school pond was a trek into imagined swampland: the grass was waist-high; the dragonflies were buzzing thick around my pigtails; and the dead log by the bank was unmistakeably an alligator. I wanted to see far more exciting creatures than the small brown frog by the waters' edge.

Mrs Clark gathered us around and poked its bottom with a pencil until it jumped away, and I have to say I wasn't really taken with her lecture about God's great ways and the perfect design of the frog for the tasks it had to do. What tasks did it have to do? And what tasks, exactly, was I made for? Was she saying God had given me my gift?

I didn't know it at the time, but that frog and I turned out to have a lot in common. Both of us were poked up the bottom in order to make us perform.

I didn't mind the act of anal sex too much. It was the way he led up to it which was upsetting, with references to getting my pipes cleaned and was I in the mood for chocolate milk tonight? And it was always the night before a show, because he swore blind that it made me a better singer, tightened my voice up that little bit, made me sing it out more clearly.

If God gave me my voice then Davie took it away again. A few years of that, and I couldn't get near a stage without having an attack of diarrhoea. Davie knew it was over, and he left with a younger model. So much for long-term management.

At that point I started collecting frogs.

33

I'm not talking about real frogs. Real frogs jump and ribbit and do all sorts of things that are of no interest to me whatsoever. But my small flat - bought with the remains of the one savings account I'd kept in my own name - had a spare room without a use, and as I was walking past the charity shop on the corner I saw a patchwork frog-shaped hot water-bottle cover in the window for fifty pence. And it just so happened that I had fifty pence on me. I'm not a great believer in signs, but I do think that one should go with the gut every now and again. I bought that cover, and the book about pond life I found in the very same shop. I've been collecting ever since. 342 frog-related products later, and not one of them has given me any happiness. That's why I've decided to get a boyfriend. One who's not interested in anal sex.

The Following Thursday

And so Keith comes into this whole thing. Keith frequents *The Cow and Moon*. I don't often go there, but I went last night, specifically to see him, being the impulsive type. I put my hair up into a beehive and painted my eyes black. I even squeezed into one of my special performing frocks, but it looked awful and brought on the diarrhoea so I changed back into jeans and a tee shirt with a hopping frog in a tiara on the front. Underneath the frog were the words, 'dancing queen'. I hoped he wouldn't ask me to dance and therefore prove I had falsely advertised my charms.

He didn't, but that was because it wasn't a dance floor evening. It was a karaoke night.

An aging sex-kitten was belting out *Gypsys, Tramps and Thieves,* and that seemed to sum up the crowd quite well. Keith was in the middle of the long bench that ran underneath the window, and his friends didn't look too bad. There were five of them, all drinking pints of something brown and frothy in silence, but Keith was the pick of the bunch, with his flatter stomach and blacker hair. The rest of them looked like older versions of him after bad marriages: I wondered if they had wives at home, wearing pinnies, slapping rolling pins, slopping their dinners out to the dog.

Keith and I would never end up that way.

I approached the table and stood in front of him. He frowned, then smiled when he recognised me.

'Can I get you a drink?' I said.

'What?' he said.

I waited until the song had finished and the smattering of applause had died away into general conversation before trying again.

'A drink?'

'I'll get you one,' he said, which wasn't what I was after, but it was a pleasant development. He looked at the beer bellies of the friends on the left, then the ones on the right, and decided to crawl under the table instead. When he got back to his feet, his yellow football shirt had become untucked, and he left it hanging over his jeans. It suited him better that way.

He guided me towards the bar, his hand on my back, and ordered a pint of bitter for himself and a dry white wine for me without consultation. Obviously that was what ladies of his acquaintance drank.

'You got a job for me?' he said.

I should explain. Keith is a handyman. He does man things around my house, such as mowing the lawn and fixing drippy taps. I found him in the Yellow Pages, under H.

'Maybe,' I said, trying to be coquettish.

'Yeah?'

'Well, you do such a good job of looking after the house… I thought maybe you'd want to look after me as well.'

'Yeah?' I don't think he got it. I sipped at my wine and tried not to wince at the taste.

A new act, one of Keith's friends, was called up to the karaoke. He strutted up with the attitude and the physique of Elvis in his Vegas period, but it was Tom Jones that sprang into life through the speakers. *It's Not Unusual,* Keith's friend sang, and apparently it wasn't, because everyone looked quite bored with his bombastic performance, as if they'd seen it a few too many times.

35

Karaoke is a funny thing. Regulars have a song that they stick to – maybe because they think they resemble the singer, or that it suits their range. Or maybe it reminds them of the one good time they had, and they're stuck like a 45 on an ancient turntable, going round and round on repeat in an attempt to maintain the illusion of standing still in that moment.

Keith's attention wavered between me and his friend on the stage. His face was tight, his moustache quivering as his lips formed the words of the song. He looked like he wanted to be up there too. He caught me watching the movement of his mouth, and shrugged.

'Wish I'd been a good singer,' he said.

'Wish I hadn't.'

'What?'

'Don't you go up there, then?' I said.

'Nah.' He looked at the stage as if it was home at the end of a long night out. 'S'magical, innit?'

I could have put up with a snorer, or a farter, or a general attitude problem. But hero-worship of light entertainment was a step too far. I downed the wine, hissed at the taste, and took a step back. 'I should get going.'

'Yeah... what was this job?'

'Doesn't matter.'

He looked hard at me. 'You all right, love?'

'It's been a bad week,' I said. 'And I thought...'

'Look, stop here for a minute, okay? Keep me company. The lads are always on at me to sing, and I don't sing. S'nice to have someone else to talk to.'

I nodded, and he ordered me another drink – vodka and orange this time, more to my taste. We were getting to know each other already. We had nothing in common apart from the fact that singing wasn't on the agenda, but that was all I needed.

Later, he walked me home and kissed me on the cheek.

The Thursday After That

'S'packed,' said Keith as he came back from the bar bearing a pint of bitter and a margarita. We'd got there early and commandeered a small round table at the back of the room, far from the stage but close to the speakers. 'S'only ever busy on Thursday nights and Saturday afternoons.'

'Why Saturday afternoons?'

'Footie,' he said. He pulled at his shirt – the yellow one with green stripes again.

'Is that your team?' I asked him.

'Brazil,' he said. 'I don't really have a team. I like the best players. Brazil's the best. Well, they were.'

'Do you mean Pele?'

He nodded and inclined his head as if impressed that a woman could know such things. I'd taken a wild guess, but he didn't need to know that. 'But there are lots of other players, brilliant players, people don't know about. Brazilian league football is the best in the world. Shits on the Premier League. Sorry. I get excited when I talk about football.'

'Right,' I said.

'You can ask me anything,' he said. 'League tables. Player stats. It's a hobby of mine.'

'It's good to have a hobby,' I said, thinking about my spare room bursting with fake frogs. Keith seemed to get a lot more out of his obsession than I did out of mine. 'Your hobby sounds great.'

'Really? You're the first person to say that.'

There was a round of applause as the first act of the night took the stage. It was a girl who couldn't have been more than sixteen under the glittered and teased hair and blue eyeliner. From her raised position on the stage, her tiny silver sequin skirt no longer hid her purple thong. All the men in the room crouched a little.

She sang Nilsson's *Without You*. The voice wasn't bad but she was too young for such a song. Somebody should have told her that there are songs which are only suitable for the old and broken amongst us. I could have done justice to *Without You*. I could have sung it to death.

Keith continued to talk away, and I nodded in the appropriate places even though I couldn't hear a thing. Occasionally, between songs, I gathered that he was telling me about football. On his face was the most beautiful expression. I wondered if he had ever been allowed to just chatter about the thing that consumed him before. When a person is a singer, everyone wants them to open their mouth. When a person is a football obsessive, everyone wants them to shut up. It didn't seem fair to me, so I let him talk, and enjoyed the way his eyes rolled and his hands fluttered like butterflies around his pint glass.

The night passed, broken into bite-sized pieces by the same old songs that people never seem to get enough of hearing. Keith's friend murdered *It's Not Unusual* again, and the aging sex kitten belted out *Gypsys, Tramps and Thieves* once more. I found myself singing a little, under my breath, at a volume that only dogs could hear. It felt good. Everything about the evening felt good. And Keith looked better than ever.

'And then, in 1926, Palestra Italia-SP came top of the Campeonato Paulista,' Keith said, 'winning all nine of their games and scoring a staggering thirty-three goals.'

'Last song of the evening!' shouted a voice. Keith stopped talking and looked up. I turned around in my seat. Keith's friend was on the stage, the microphone in his hand and a dangerous, beery grin on his fat face. 'Please welcome... Keith and friend!'

The crowd gave half-hearted applause which stepped up a gear as the rest of Keith's friends, at their usual table, whooped and stamped their feet.

'Shit,' said Keith.

'I really can't,' I said. 'Really. I can't.'

'Christ.' The crowd kept clapping. The friend on the stage put down the microphone and pushed through to stand in front of our small table. 'C'mon, Keith!' he shouted. 'Give us a duet with your lady friend.'

'Oh no no,' I said.

'Keith shook his head and folded his arms. The crowd clapped harder, starting shouting. There was a sense of inevitability in the air as Keith's shoulders drooped. He stood up, tucked his yellow football shirt into his jeans, and offered his hand to me.

'I really can't,' I said. I could feel my bowels rumbling.

'Come on.' In his eyes I could see desperation, a plea to accompany him up to that place he idolised and feared in equal measure. Alone, he could not conquer it. But together, we stood a chance. Maybe the same was true for me too. Apart we could only be silent, but as a couple, we could sing a song, and do it justice.

I stood up.

The crowd made mad noises, like animals in the zoo awaiting feeding time, as we stepped on to the stage. I've performed in front of some rowdy groups in clubs and bars, but this one took my breath away. The introduction to the song started to play, and they quietened, but their expressions were still hungry, their eyes trained on us as if they were the lions and we were fresh meat.

Don't Go Breaking My Heart.

Keith sang first, took the opening line, hit one note out of six and was out of time, but at least he'd got the words out and had maintained a decent volume, and then it was my turn.

'I couldn't if I tried!' I sang: every note was perfect, like bluebird song, and I laced my arm around Keith's waist and gave a little shimmy and a wink, feeling the urge to sing out sweep back over me like I'd been swiped with a great big glittery brush from God, who had made me to perform just like he'd made frogs to jump.

Keith stopped singing and looked at me with open mouth, so I sang his lines as well. He recovered by the chorus, and did a fair job of harmonising. With some practice on his part, we might have been okay. Kiki Dee's not really my kind of range, but it was pleasant to sing something light and undemanding, and Keith's presence next to me made it easy to shine. The song passed as quick as an eyeblink, and when I looked around the room everyone was applauding me, whistling, shaking their heads in amazement.

Everyone apart from Keith.

He stared at me. 'What's that smell?' he said.

'I'm so sorry,' I said. 'I've shat myself.'

39

Not the Next Thursday, But the Thursday After That

I put on a black wig, Cleopatra-style, and the darkest sunglasses I could find to brave *The Cow and Moon*. It took a lot to walk back through those doors, but it was pointless anyway – he wasn't there. Something told me he would never be there again.

The regulars sang the same old songs. Nobody bought me a drink. Nobody asked me to sing. It was for the best, really.

On the way home I passed the enormous 24 hour Tesco's and wandered through the car park and up to the sliding doors. I kidded myself I wanted some biscuits, a treat from the expensive range, maybe Belgian chocolate cookies or those German wafers with hearts on the packet, but really I knew where I wanted to go. I headed for the toy section, hoping to catch a glimpse of green.

They had a new range in stuffed toys. Fairy Tale Furries, they were called, and amongst the bears and the pigs and the wolves in grandmother-style caps, were long thin frogs with red smiles. I picked one up and held it in my hands. It wore a gauzy skirt, and when I turned it over the skirt flipped over its head to reveal a golden-haired prince underneath, complete with dashing moustache and enormous crown. He looked like a real catch.

I paid for the Frog Prince and took him home. Instead of banishing him into the spare room, I took him into bed with me and put him next to me on the pillow. After I'd turned out the light, I could feel his presence beside me, reaching out to me, begging me to take him in my hands and make him into a man once more.

Mrs Clarke was wrong. God doesn't design us perfectly for the tasks we are meant to undertake. God makes blobs, and the blobs divide and become creatures, and creatures become different as time goes on because they don't want to stay the same, to keep repeating the same tasks again and again.

I might have to kiss a lot of frogs before I find a prince who can make me into a princess. But I'll keep kissing away. I have a feeling that inside all of us frogs who are fed up of jumping to the same tune, there are human beings.

LEGO LAND

Lego. It's amazing stuff.

It can be used to build anything.

Robert built a Lego world and kept it in his basement, suspended from the ceiling on a piece of wool picked from the sleeve of his third favourite pullover. He built the world in sections: a core, tectonic plates, a crust, and then continents, countries, mountains, volcanoes, the occasional tree. It wasn't the most hospitable planet to look at but that was for a reason. Robert had been elbowed on the crowded underground platform on his way to work once too often. Now he wanted a planet to himself.

So it was an annoyance when the tiny aliens moved in.

He suspected they had been there for some time, but the first he knew of it was when they started changing things. They built Lego structures, only just visible to the naked eye, which turned out to be city-like constructions, clusters of long, thin buildings, rather like multicoloured skyscrapers. Robert watched them through his new powerful microscope, paid for by the remortgage. These cities were the hubs of activity, but the miniscule creatures were everywhere, living in Lego tepees or igloos in some places and Lego mansions in others; it seemed equality did not have a place on planet Robert.

The aliens were really quite sweet in appearance. They had little yellow heads, green bellies and six pairs of beautiful blue eyes. Their legs and feelers were white. They reminded Robert of the sand-hoppers he had seen once on a day trip to Weston Supermare, but these aliens had mouths that were entirely human – red lips, strong white teeth, even tiny pink tongues that waggled.

The cities grew bigger and bigger. The changes were visible to the naked eye, and it became obvious where the material for these buildings was coming from. Large empty craters appeared on the surface of the planet. It seemed the aliens were mining Lego, and had found a way to chop it down into smaller pieces that they could manipulate in order to create their structures. The craters grew in size every day.

And then the spaceship appeared.

Robert accidentally stepped on it where it lay, on the bottom stair in his basement. He heard it crunch under his foot, and looked down to see a red and white rocket, built from tiny pieces of Lego, smaller than his little fingernail, with the cone broken in two. He estimated it must have held at least a thousand of the aliens, and with the rush of guilt came the pins and needles on the back of his neck that he always experienced when he was really annoyed. Why did he have to care for these unwanted invaders? It was his basement, and his planet, to do with what he wished. Right now he wished to be alone, and in order to do that he would have to commit planetocide.

So much for personal space.

He walked out, shut the door, turned the key, and tried hard not to think about the aliens for the next month. Life returned to normal. He got elbowed five times on the underground platform, ignored by the women he attempted to smile at on a daily basis, and passed over for promotion at work. He bought a Playstation but found the games a little too violent for him. He went to a speed dating evening and talked to a blonde nurse who gave him her number but then never returned his call. He turned on the television but for some reason the reception was terrible, and the cable was wired up in the basement, so in the end he decided to take up reading books, and before he knew it he'd started reading science fiction, and aliens were in his head again. So, one long, lonely evening, after he had finished the complete works of Arthur C Clarke and there was nothing else to do, he turned the key, opened the door, and ventured down the stairs once more.

They were waiting for him.

Millions of tiny lights glittered on the face of the planet, diffused into soft twinkles by fine strands, resembling cobwebs that spun out from the globe face to connect with various items in the basement. There was a concentration of the lines between the fuse box and the cable network box; it appeared that those objects had grown unkempt beards.

Tiny red and white rockets littered the floor. There were perhaps fifty, perhaps more.

Robert hesitated on the bottom stair, his eyes fixed on the lights, which, unbelievably had been arranged into a pattern that was undoubtedly a message: a message in English.

HI

He went back up the stairs into the kitchen, turned on the kettle and then sat down on the linoleum. Everything seemed to have become a little scary, and the cold hard diamond pattern felt reassuring against his hands and bottom, making it easier to think. How could they have gained power? Perhaps the fine strands were stealing energy from the wiring in the basement. If that was so, his electricity bill was going to be enormous.

But that couldn't explain their ability to understand his language, or their apparent desire to communicate. Maybe they had been receiving information through the cable network? Had they been watching television? At any rate, the effort involved in making that sign of greeting must have been enormous. He imagined that a human message that large would have required making fifty or so lights, each the size of Wales. Incredible.

He decided that kind of exertion deserved a response.

He got up, dusted his bottom with his hands, and took down the permanently unused white board from next to the telephone, along with a marker pen. Then he went back down into the basement.

The message was still there. Robert stood on his habitual spot, the bottom stair, and wrote out a one-word response on his white board. He held it up towards the planet.

HELLO

Instantly, the message on the face of the Lego blinked off, and a new one replaced it.

WHO ARE U

How had they made such massive changes so quickly? Perhaps time did not move in a similar way on their planet. Certainly their life cycles had to be shorter. How long did sand hoppers live for, anyway? Robert made a mental note to look it up as he rubbed out his word and considered what he would write next.

He opted for the truth.

THE CREATOR

The words looked good in black and white. He felt quite emotional when he imagined what effect they must be causing amongst the aliens down there on planet Robert.

The lights on the planet winked off and were not immediately replaced. Robert wondered how many years had passed down there. Maybe thousands.

The next question surprised him somewhat.

Y R WE HERE

At first the free and easy text messaging style of language annoyed him, but then it occurred to him that they were probably just trying to cut down on a phenomenal work load, so he forgave them. It seemed they had forgotten that they had arrived from someplace else initially. Perhaps they'd misplaced some records. It wasn't as if he had any answers, but it didn't seem right for the Creator to admit that, so he opted for a remark he occasionally made at work when a colleague asked him a difficult question.

DON'T YOU KNOW?

Their message was replaced instantly with another.

NO

He wrote his response in tiny letters and hoped they could read it.

WELL IF YOU DON'T KNOW YOU CAN'T EXPECT ME TO TELL YOU

The lights on the planet went off and stayed off.

Robert sat down and picked at the rubber soles of his slippers. How long had he been down here? He decided he quite fancied a cup of tea, so he went upstairs and made one. After a few sips he felt that he wanted a biscuit, so he retrieved a custard cream from the barrel in the cupboard next to the sink and made it last by eating one corner at a time. Then he finished his tea, picked up his white board and marker pen, and went back downstairs.

The message had changed.

WOT DO WE DO

That was a tricky one. Robert thought hard. Luckily the tea had had a revitalising effect and it wasn't long before he decided on an answer.

BE NICE TO EACH OTHER

He was fairly pleased with his response. It was a motto he personally wished more people would live by, and he didn't feel it wasn't too prescriptive or demanding. Maybe his words would make Planet Lego a really marvellous place to be. For the first time he wished he'd put in a few more trees and made a few less volcanoes. The sand hopper alien beings deserved a place with a bit more greenery.

If only there was some way he could shrink himself and go amongst them. He wanted to live there, in a place where nobody elbowed anybody else or forgot to return calls. Maybe they could develop the technology to shrink him? They seemed like an immensely bright bunch of aliens. He was writing out a message indicating his desire to visit them, if they could think of way to arrange it, when all the lights in the basement, even the one naked bulb above his head, went out.

A moment later the planet exploded into a million tiny flames.

The orange flickering was like a strobe effect; soundless, and so bright it hurt Robert's eyes. It lasted for about a minute. Tiny wisps of smoke drifted up and made a fog that dissipated as the long thin strands from the fuse box and cable box floated gently downwards to lie on the floor of the basement.

'Oh,' Robert said. He appeared to have started a world war.

He considered writing a message, but he couldn't think of anything to say. He thought about enquiring if everything was all right down there, but wondered if it might do more harm than good.

Still, he was sure they could rebuild. Given time, surely they would forget his intervention and he could go back to watching them from a distance. Maybe this war was for the best. He'd learned his lesson – this time round he'd make sure they didn't wire themselves up to the electricity grid.

He was just beginning to feel positive about the whole affair when the strand of wool, the one from sleeve of his third favourite pullover, snapped.

The world smacked down on the concrete floor and smashed apart.

'Oh,' Robert said again. There didn't seem to be much else to say.

He turned around, walked up the stairs, closed the basement door, turned the key, and went into the living room. He sat in his favourite armchair and picked Lego from his clothes and out of his hair.

Maybe he'd hand in his notice tomorrow. One could hardly go back to being a customer services representative after one had been a God.

He'd start work on a new planet instead. One with more trees, a few scenic lakes, a play park and a couple of coffee shops.

And he'd use something stronger than wool to hold it in position.

THE BENGALO BOYS

There has always been death in my hand. My grandmother saw it there when I was a baby, and palms do not change. Nowadays I don't look at the lines any more, the ones on my hand or on my face. They only tell me what I already know. Those boys were marked on me from the beginning, and I have only tonight to put them to rest.

The fire is getting low in the grate and the chill of the evening is seeping under the window sash and into my joints. Olivia is upstairs, of course, in the bedroom that we share. The air will smell of her when I enter at nine, as is my custom. I will breathe in the odour of her dirty nightgown, the urine and bedsores.

Olivia has been in that room for five years. She did not ask me if I would care for her: change her bedpan and her sheets, rub cream into her cracked, papery thighs, but I did these things just the same. I always have.

But no more.

In the darkened hall, the grandfather clock strikes eight. He is late, but I do not doubt that he is coming. As a charity worker, it is his duty to attend to the weak, the sick, the old, and I am all three. I pull back the net across the window, rub away a patch of condensation, and look out over the street. These terraced houses are small, and I imagine the bricks straining to contain the life within. There are young families, their faces swimming in the blue warmth of the television screen, drinking up life, thinking there will always be more.

The headlamps on the cars passing by are blurs that frighten me. When the familiar white van comes to a halt in front of my house I have to search for the confidence to stand still and watch Gordon emerge under the streetlight.

The fire is almost out. I add a scoop of coal and then brave the chill of the hallway to open the front door. Gordon gives me his professional smile, the one I imagine he practises in the bathroom mirror after he cleans his off-white teeth every morning, and I step aside to let him pass. He knows the way.

He takes the seat furthest from the fire. 'Well, Doris, what was so important that you had to see me tonight?'

I sit down and fold my hands in my lap. 'Olivia's dead,' I say. 'She died this evening. In her sleep.'

He stares at me. I expected him to attempt to take charge: to tell me that we must phone an ambulance, check the body, make ourselves busy to ward off reality. Instead he surprises me with his quiet nod and anxious mouth.

'That's terrible,' he says. 'I… oh dear, Doris. What can I do to help?'

'Do you remember when I read your palm?'

'Well, um, yes. Yes I do. You said you saw a journey to a faraway place. And a family. Boys, you said. Two boys.'

'That's not all I saw.' I clear my throat and put on my gypsy voice, the high, crooning one that I used to use when Olivia and I worked in the business. The Bengalo Sisters, we were. *See the future with the Bengalos. Cross their palms and they'll call forth the spirits.* 'You have the gift.'

'Sorry?'

'The gift of second sight. I saw it in your hand. I need to call forth spirits, you see. It has to be tonight.'

I get up and move to the cabinet. I take down my velvet, and the silver candlestick holder which holds an unburned candle. It is years since I made these preparations, but they come back to me easily. The velvet slides over the coffee table and the candlestick sits in the middle of the velvet. I fetch the matches from the mantelpiece and light the candle.

'Doris, I think maybe we should be thinking about calling the authorities, or something,' Gordon says. 'There'll be plenty to do.'

'You said you'd help.' I turn off the lamp and we are left in the yellow glow of the candle, radiating out from the centre of the table. The velvet underneath it soaks up most of the light. With my

49

old eyes it is difficult to see Gordon's expression. It's his voice that tells me he is beginning to feel afraid.

'Yes, but I meant with the arrangements.'

'This is my last chance,' I say, and the quiver in my throat is real. 'It has to be now. Please.'

'I'm only a charity worker,' he says. 'I don't know anything about…'

'Take my hands.' I sit back in my chair and hold out my hands, palms up, on either side of the candle. The first drops of wax spill over and pool on the velvet.

Gordon takes my hands.

A lot of what we used to do was fakery. I'll admit that. The flickering lights, the wavering voices – all designed to get us more believers, more money. There was never enough money, and sometimes Olivia had to work in the night, taking favours from men, to make ends meet. She always was the brave one, the one that gave the orders. But her gift was real. I had a little of it, for the reading of palms and suchlike, but Olivia could reach through the layers of death like brushing aside a soft curtain. Perhaps that was why she found death such an easy thing to accept. She faced her own, and the deaths of others, without a qualm.

Gordon has soft palms, a little damp, and his grip is uncertain so I grab on to him tightly and call out to other side before he can pull away.

'Spirits, we speak to you. Spirits, we ask you to draw near to us. Spirits, come to us now!'

There is silence.

Gordon breathes out, soft and low.

The fire in the grate flickers.

The candle goes out.

'They're here,' I say. The temperature of the room has dropped. I can see Gordon's breath as it forms, to hang from his lips and dissipate with each exhalation.

'Now, I should really get going. My wife…'

'They want to talk to you.'

He gives a nervous laugh. 'Really, I, think I should...'

The fire roars up in a sheet of crackling orange that shouts down his words. He stops and stares at the flames.

'Who's there?' I ask. 'Who is it?'

The net curtain whispers as it moves, as if a hand has been run down its length.

Gordon's eyes are huge and white. His grip tightens on mine, to the point of pain. 'I can hear them. Like a room full of people, all talking at once, standing in a huge chamber, the echoes going around and around... How are you doing this?'

I shake my head. 'Not me. You. You're doing it.'

'But I never –'

'You need to concentrate. Try not to listen to them all. Search through the crowds.'

'Who for?' He closes his eyes. 'Olivia?'

'No!' I pray he has not begun to focus on my sister, on her image. She must not come, not tonight. 'Not her. Look for the children. They will be near, I promise. They have always been near.'

Those boys have followed me as if I was their mother, through all these years. I know it. Sometimes I'll catch a high call on the wind, or a giggle in the popping of the fire. Shiny things have moved of their own accord: my hair slides, my mother of pearl-backed mirror. Olivia said I was imagining it, but I could see the lie in her eyes. The boys were there, and she refused to talk to them for these past forty years. She pretended they never existed.

Gordon snaps opens his eyes and looks around me, to the sides of my chair, at the level of my shoulder. He smiles. 'You're right. They are near. They are standing around you. Calling to you. They call you...'

'Auntie,' I whispered.

'Yes, that's right. Auntie Doris,' Gordon says. 'Auntie Doris, they say, come and play.'

'Not yet. Tell them not yet. Will you ask them something?'

'They say mother is near.' Gordon frowns. 'They're afraid. They have to go.'

51

'No! Ask them if they forgive me. Please...I didn't want to hurt them. Olivia made me. She said she'd lose the gift if she had children...that I had to get rid of them with the coat hanger. She told me it wasn't wrong, but I knew it was. I knew it. I've waited so long to be forgiven...'

Gordon squeezes my hands and throws his eyes up to the ceiling. 'No...'

The curtain twitches and the fire shrinks down. The room is so cold.

'Please,' I beg, one last time, but Gordon doesn't reply. His eyes are still fixed on the ceiling.

'She's angry,' he says. 'She's so angry with you.'

His hands drop away from mine.

'I had to. My time is up. I can see it in my palm, don't you understand? This is my last chance to be forgiven so that I can join them, take care of them. But they have to welcome me, not run away; they have to call as I cross over so that I can find them. Olivia wouldn't help me – she wouldn't let me call. Not while there was a breath in her body, she said.'

'It wasn't her time,' Gordon says. 'She's not ready to go. She says she's staying. She is so angry with you. She says she's staying for you.'

Loud, against the wood of the bedroom floorboards – a knock.

The fire goes out.

The candle goes out.

I can barely make out Gordon, slumped in the chair, unmoving. A faint, no doubt, just like Olivia used to suffer. She collapsed after every performance, and came round a few minutes later. He'll be fine.

The chill of the evening has left my joints numb, and it takes me two tries to get to my feet. I pat Gordon on the cheek as I pass him, and savour the warmth of skin against mine one last time. Then I shuffle along the hallway and look up the staircase to the landing, and the door of the bedroom where Olivia waits for me.

Is that the sound of a child in the rattle of the letterbox as the wind blows it back and forth on its hinges? Or is it my imagination?

'Olivia,' I say. 'I'm coming.'

And then I climb the stairs.

LEGS

I have an agoraphobic neighbour. She has her legs removed due to diabetes. The forced trip to the hospital cures her agoraphobia. The neighbour's husband dies. Now she only has a burning edge on her - the need to be out and about in her wheelchair, facing the world full on. She develops a paranoia that her arms are going to drop off. She becomes so depressed that she would not be able to get up in the morning if she was capable of getting up in the morning.

The caring faceless ones appoint a regular visitor to make her partake in life. He is Lovely Young Man. On his first visit she asks him to take her outside. He slips on a dog turd in the park and lets go of the wheelchair handles. Park Hill, I should say; the heavily sloping grass covered with friendly squirrels who leap aside as the neighbour flies past. She would scream but she swallowed a gnat on the way down and is still trying to cough it up when she hits the main road.

Robbed of her last scream. Her earlier life was really fabulous, though. She once went on a day trip to Blackpool and wowed the locals. She had the photograph framed in her living room.

I know, because I went in with a card I had picked out reluctantly after her operation. I plumped for, "Hope You Are Feeling Better." She thanked me with insulted, wet old eyes and her husband moved slightly in his corner armchair. It may very well have been the last movement he made. He was dead two days later, and after that he was dead for another day before he became ambulance/hospital/burial/officially dead. Assigned to die, like his wife's legs. At least he got a burial. Her legs were incinerated. At least, that's what the caring faceless ones told her.

I met Angry Young Man clearing out the house after the second funeral, during which, appropriately, he had gotten legless. His loveliness had been robbed. He was harsh and sandpapery. We went for a top-up drink and I liked him. I liked his self-absorption.

54

It's not every day you meet an atoning murderer who keeps a mangled wheelchair on his wall as a constant reminder of himself. I told him he had done nothing wrong; I had done worse things deliberately, and they had never jarred on me the way his crimes covered him. They rustled softly through his voice. Soothing.

Why did it continue to bother him? How could he find the consistency to care?

My interest lasted a few weeks. But he started talking about death in bed and I knew he had to go. So, no close knit harmonious relationship between us, then, but the weight of knowing someone's worst guilt. It tied me to him, and I followed him through the next five years of his urtication by a series of postcards that he sent to me.

> *Working for British Rail - am in Hell.*
> *Have taken up Karate. Still thinking about it.*
> *Three years ago today. Am television researcher.*
> *Trying to move on. Tenerife is hot.*
> *Making a fresh start.*

This one was a genuine surprise to me, even more so because he had a written a reply address in careless letters at the bottom of the cartoon postcard. It seemed he considered it my duty to reply. Why is it, when people move on from something they are ashamed of, they want to visit it once more from their new perspective? What is the urge to kick the corpse?

But I did what was expected of me. I wrote a polite letter on blue paper that prompted him for more information, and between us we arranged a meeting in a pub that was local for him, and a long drive away for me. He wanted to call all the shots and my life wasn't interesting enough for me to refuse him.

I won't repeat the conversation we had. Conversations have so many boring stumbling blocks as people search for what they want to hear. Both egos to be flattered, and both desires to be hidden. I've no doubt that what he told me that day, after the obligatory four pints to loosen his nerve and his tongue, wasn't the truth anyway.

But I shall tell you for the sake of a story, and I shall remove all the parts that could easily have been replaced with bleating noises.

He said that he had travelled after my rejection of him. That he saw the reason for pushing him away, and it had only been the very start of the relationship, and it shouldn't have hurt as much as it did, but that it had, and so he had left the town and tried on a score of different towns for size.

Chester had been quaint. The British Rail tea shop he had been working in had been battered with sledge hammers when it was erected in 1967 to give it an old, surviving look. People had taken to it, and requested strong tea and lardy cake instead of the obligatory burger. Angry young man had lost the edge of his anger through his shifts behind the counter. Instead, as he realised how eager everyone was to encourage the lie that this rail station was a shining example of Merrie Olde England, he had slipped painfully to depressed young man. Postcard Number One.

So he moved to the big cough. London. Strictly speaking, to a town that was an hour from Piccadilly Circus by tube but as it had a tube stop, was called London. There he used his unemployment benefit to strengthen his muscles through Karate. He worked hard and long at it to change his body completely: there could be no doubt about it after six months of continuous workouts, that this was a man who would not let go of a little old lady's wheelchair handles in any situation. The size of his arm muscles began to deny his own past, but he wasn't prepared to put it down. Not yet. No matter what his body said. Postcard Number Two.

Three years have passed in his story, and to him it is known as the third year anniversary. Not a healthy way to be, he thinks. He buries himself in knowledge by taking a job devising questions for a quiz show, and trying to memorise every single one he prepares. He tops up his income by entering local pub quizzes until he is banned from them all. Then, because the job can be done at a long distance as easily as a short one, he relocates to Scotland. The very northern tip of Scotland. He wears extra woolly jumpers to the one pub quiz he can find until he gets banned from that, too. What could possibly take up his time now? He has a lot of time to spend shivering and alone in which to find out. Postcard Number Three.

An idea begins to form, and to encourage it to germinate he takes a long holiday in the Canaries. The heat turns his now beautiful body a golden cherry colour. He looks new, brand new, just out of the packaging, white teeth glinting new. Sexual acrobatics become a game he perfects, and in the aftermath of a thousand women the idea is born. A proper future. One he could face every day from now on that would be an emphatic rebuttal of that one moment he let define him. Postcard Number Four.

He will become a medical student. And that, in turn, will turn him into a Doctor. A good one. One that saves lives through constant care and consideration. He knows now that he is intelligent enough to survive in that world, and maybe it could even convince him that the death he caused was for a reason. The reason being that it all led him here. Postcard Number Five.

I was about to congratulate him on his noble journey when he continued to speak. He was well into initial training now, and was busily getting used to the smell and texture of the dead as he examined and dissected them. It all offered no immediate problem: that was, until three days ago, when he had been presented with his first leg.

It was old, yellow, stinking of formaldehyde, and cut off precisely at the thigh. The thickness of the ankle and the unique blue marble pattern of the varicose veins gave the sex and age away, and like the sudden clapping of hands from an angry teacher, he is convinced that the leg is hers. You know who. The crackling skin accuses him. The horned toenails stare him down.

His entire body turned colder than it had ever felt in Scotland, and then hotter that it had ever burnt in Tenerife. But he was a harder man - one that was used to his own accusations, and before he had time to crawl off and think for another five years, he had picked up a scalpel and cut deeply into the calf muscle, burrowing inside it to find the veins and bone, just like the rest of the class.

In that moment, all guilt and shame vanished.

Don't ask me why. I don't know why. He couldn't explain it either. But he is well on the way to becoming anything from an awful to a passable doctor, and I have nothing else to say.

If I was feeling particularly honest I would add that I had asked him if he wanted to go out to eat after our final pint, and he had turned me down with a superior, concerned smile on his face. If I could have told him that I had only been after one night of cheap and meaningless sex to dissolve our ties I would have, but I could not face the words. Besides, he was happy to think that I wanted him back forever, that it was my turn to face my own mistake.

I can't call him Angry Young Man anymore. I can call him, in the past tense of no longer knowing him, Well Adjusted Young Man. Adjusted to life, adjusted to death, and adjusted to the purpose of legs.

FLUSHED

There's an awful moment in any friendship when it becomes obvious that you no longer like each other.

Pop quiz, hotshot. What do you do?

- Call it a day
- Pretend nothing has happened and carry on meeting up at the pub every Friday, changing talk to reminiscences about the great times you had rather than attempting to find a new topic.

I go for option two. I act friendly. It all sounds friendly in my head. But I can't let this important moment, the death of our friendship, go by without alluding to it. I'm the kind of person that has to point out that the prize fish in the tank is dead, you see. I have to tell you the toilet paper is caught on your heel or I just can't rest.

'Hey, Pippa,' I say, 'More booze? I'll get them in. Club later? Toppers? Shufties? Curly fries and cheese to follow it all up? Remember that great night in Chester? Brilliant. Shame those days are all gone. Behind us. Don't you feel like it's a real shame?'

'Yeah, it sucks,' she says. She has an umbrella-topped drink in each claw and is taking turns sipping them. 'Being over twenty is like being a bit dead, innit?'

'It's not just that. It's like, also that thing you said about my mum.'

'What?'

'My mum. When you said that you hated her.'

'Yeah, but you said you hated her first.'

'That doesn't make it right!' I shout, and suddenly there are tears and wobbly movements to the loo, pushing past the long queue of sparkly heifers giving it mouth – *whaddya think you're there's a queue here you get to the frigging* – you know what I mean.

God, the Pussycat Dolls are loud and mean on the ears. The sound reverberates around the five stalls and three sinks, and the floor is sticky under stiletto. I hate my life – it hits me just like that. I hate my life, and my mum, and I know this is meant to be a gradual process of realisation but it's not, it's like a great big fucking Frankenstein monster of a turnaround in my head.

The other girls push past me and give me evils. Sheree comes out of the nearest stall and her hair is this incredible pink mess. She's even found a lipstick in the same shade, unbelievably; I thought that went out twenty years ago, so maybe she's borrowed her mum's. I bet she has a good relationship with her mum. I bet they talk about types of condom and everything.

Just the thought of it is enough to set me off again, so I dive into the stall Sheree just came out of and squat down on the floor, next to the sanitary towel disposal box, and wonder why I'm such a disaster zone and how exactly the floors of toilets always manage to end up so sticky. What's on them? Is it wee? Are women so drunk that they fall off the seat and end up pissing all over the floor as they lie on their backs and kick their legs like giant cockroaches?

Not a good image.

'Hello.....'

The voice has a deep resonance, as if coming from an underground cavern.

'Hello?' I say.

'Hello, Tanya...'

'Hello?' I sit up and look around the cubicle.

'Down here.'

'Where?'

'In the hole.' The voice drops even lower, and gives a creepy laugh, as if it's in a second rate horror film. 'The hole, Tanya. The hole... mwah ha ha ha ha...' I peer into the toilet. There is no water. The smooth off-white bowl drops away to a star-speckled galaxy, and in the centre of the unimaginable millions of miles of emptiness is a small pink duck. Not a real one, obviously. A cartoon character representation of one.

'You're a duck,' I said.

'No, I'm a being of vast power.'

'You look a lot like a duck.'

'I'm being kind on your eyes. If I showed you the real me, it would blind you instantly.'

'Yeah, well, I can manage that too if I forget to put my make-up on.' I eyeball him. 'So what's up, duck?'

'Tanya,' it boomed, 'your life is shit. Come to terms with your hatred of your mother, stop drinking too much in disgusting nightclubs, and try harder to impress boys, and you could unlock your deep, deep potential.'

'I have potential?' It was news to me.

A banging on the door drowned out the duck's answer. 'Busy!' I shouted. The banging stopped. 'You know, this is a drug-related moment. I've ingested something. Some oik must have slipped me Rohypnol.'

'If that was true you'd be asleep in the back of a taxi, heading for a not very nice flat and an appointment with a video camera, methinks. No, trust me, Tanya, this is real.'

'No shit,' I say, and then remember I'm talking to a toilet and have a laugh at my own wit.

'I'm wasted here,' says the duck. It sighs. 'Right, look, just try to be a better person, okay? Before it's too late. And it's very nearly too late. Disaster is around the corner.'

'I'll try,' I say, in a reassuring tone. I've used it on my mum before when she's obsessing about the length of my skirts, as if that meant anything to anyone other than the pre-naughties generation. Or standing in the living room at 2.30 in the morning, telling me I'm a disgrace. And then I'm crying again. 'I hate my mum,' I say. 'I hate my mum and my life.'

'No,' says the duck, patiently, 'you just hate yourself.'

'That's so not deep on any level.' I have a think about it, then as quick as I can give my state of inebriation, I lift my skirt, pull down my pants, sit on the toilet, and have a wee. Then, while the duck is still coughing, I flush.

61

'Byeeee,' I say, over the scream and the gurgle.

The banging starts again on the door, so I get myself presentable and then throw back the door to have a right go at the stick-girl on the other side. She backs off quick-smart; they always do if you make eye-contact in the right way.

On the dance floor, the Pussycats have seceded to Alesha Dixon, and all the girls are out there, waggling their fingers at their imaginary boyfriends who do nothing. Pippa is out there too, with Carlie and Kylie and Candida. What a happy little groupette, in a circle, no gaps to be muscled into, no room for one more.

So I leave.

Outside, the air is very cold and the electric lights turn the night into a kind of purple haze, so the song starts playing in my mind and it's the best sound to stomp home to. I could be a rock chick. I could wear black and only eat black foods and think black. That would be easy for me, particularly with my new mum-hating, world-hating vibe going on, but I decide against it. I'm not sure why.

I get home, and the house is darker than the street. Usually mum waits up so she can say something awful. I swear she spends hours thinking it up, but tonight the walls are not hot with her plottings. It's an icy house, a dead one. The music, even the haze in my head, has stopped.

The lounge is abandoned, the telly turned off at the wall and a Dairy Milk wrapper next to a nearly empty cup of hot chocolate, the brown smeared over the rim, mingling with that peculiar pink of her lipstick.

The kitchen is worse: the dirty plates, the crumpled washing still in the basket. The hall echoes with my footsteps. The stairs shrink up and away to an awful epiphany.

She's gone.

The duck warned me, and I didn't listen, and she went. This is what truly alone is, this feeling, now – the house without meaning, and nobody to tell you that you're disappointing them.

I go up the stairs. I pass her bedroom door. It's closed. I make it to my own bedroom with wobbly little steps, and I take off my clothes to a mantra: could-she-have-left-could-she-have-left-could-she-have-left? Really?

I tell myself that in the morning she'll be there. She's in her bedroom now. Asleep. I could go and check. I could get up and go and see her, eyes closed, on her side, denting the mattress, fat chin on the pillow.

The duck said I should trust myself.

Trust me, I say, she's there. It's not too late to make everything right, to start over, to make the most of my potential. It still sounds stupid and Hollywood and pretty much impossible, but I have to believe it now, or else my life has gone the way of the duck. Flushed away.

I lie awake, and wait until the new morning, and try to trust.

SONGS FOR DEAD CHILDREN

I walked into the party and was met with silence. I don't remember feeling anything; all my guilt and despair had already leaked out of me, in the dressing room, after the performance.

Guido greeted me with a kiss on each cheek. He wore a purple velvet suit and a bow tie, and his corkscrew hair was held back from his face by a plastic multicoloured band that might suit a young girl. 'Our star,' he said, and then, 'have you seen the reviews? Never mind, never mind. Critics. I'll get you a champagne.'

He pushed into the sombre crowd. People looked at me, then at each other. Appropriately, it felt like a funeral was in progress. I looked up at the low ceiling, covered in yellowed tiles, and the wooden surround from which hung paintings of Von Karajan, Von Dingelstedt, and of Mahler himself. The elegant auditorium had been cavernous, a black hole I attempted to fill with my voice, and yet this back room was tiny, squashed full of red and gold furniture and a hundred different perfumes, overwhelming, yet all smelling only of money. Von Karajan raised his nose and his baton over them all; Mahler looked forlorn to find himself in their company.

I heard Guido ordering champagne at an obscenely loud volume, and I knew it had been a mistake to come at all. I could have left the country, gone home, given up my dreams rather than face having them ripped away. I made my way to the darkest corner of the room and sat in a small chair with a high back and scrolled wooden arms, hoping to be forgotten. Of course, that couldn't happen; and yet, I was grateful when the only person who found the courage to approach me was a middle-aged man with rimless glasses, a trimmed beard, and a way of holding himself that suggested he was not out to humiliate me further.

He held out a cut-glass tumbler. 'It's brandy,' he said. 'I thought that might appeal more. Make this ordeal bearable.' He had an American accent but he spoke in slow, formal sentences.

'Thank you.' I took the tumbler and held it in my lap. He sat down opposite me, in a matching chair, and I noticed the thick brown buttons on his waistcoat and the solid knot of his striped tie. 'You don't look like one of the usual crowd.'

'I'm not Viennese,' he said, 'obviously. I'm sorry, I mean, I don't live in Vienna. I travelled over from Pittsburgh.'

'On holiday?' I couldn't work out how he had ended up in this gathering; such events were never open to mere members of the public.

He gave a small grimace, then said, 'I came for the music.'

I tried to hide my disappointment. 'Then I'm sorry I let a lover of Mahler down so badly.'

'No, no...' But I could tell he was trying to be kind. He screwed up his eyes and made a hissing sound between his teeth. 'I'm handling this badly. Look, I came because it was the Kindertotenlieder. It's special to me. I don't know if anyone could do it justice, in my eyes. Do you understand?'

I gave a nod. 'I know what it is to care for a piece of music.'

'Mahler?'

'No, my first love is Mozart.'

'Ah.' He looked disappointed. 'That could explain it, of course. Why you didn't connect tonight.'

'I beg your pardon?'

His hand flew to the knot of his tie and he pulled at the material. 'I'm sorry, I didn't mean to offend...'

'No, no, you didn't,' I told him, and his honesty was suddenly the purest thing in the room to me. 'You are right. I failed to connect. But the subject matter...'

'Yes, of course! That's what I mean. Songs for dead children. How can one who loves Mozart give themselves over to the world of darkness that Mahler gives us?'

65

'Except it's not darkness,' I said. 'There arises a new sun, doesn't there? Those are the first lines.'

'Yes, and you sang them with hope, didn't you?' And I saw my first mistake. I was wrong from the beginning. The sun was not a symbol of life, after all. It was the burning face of despair, and I hadn't wanted to sing about such things. 'You're not married, Fraulein Mutter, are you?'

'No.'

'Maybe when you have children of your own this piece might make more sense to you. You are simply too young to sing it. It's a song of experience.'

'The experience of death.'

'Yes.' He looked down at his feet.

The room seemed to have emptied around us. I was aware of nothing but that moment as I leaned over to touch his arm and said, 'You... had a child that died?'

'I've lost many children.' He looked up at me. 'I'm a paediatric oncologist.'

'Yes. What a horrible job.'

He pulled back his shoulders. 'Do you think so?'

I could see I had offended him, and I was sorry for it. I said, 'This party is awful.'

'Yes.'

'I want to understand. I have an obligation to sing the Kindertotenlieder many times over the next six months. We are touring...'

'Yes.'

Guido's voice reached me, demanding to know where I was, whom I needed to meet, how I couldn't be allowed to hide away. 'Come with me to my hotel,' I said to him. 'There's a quiet bar there. We can talk some more. If you wouldn't mind.'

'Talk about the music?' he said. 'Of course.'

We made a quiet escape, leaving Guido's voice, still shouting for me, behind us, and I summoned one of the horse-drawn carriages that line the Kartnerstrasse.

66

The hotel bar was tiny: carefully lit to preserve privacy, with three small red leather booths opposite the sleek expanse of the counter and the polished order of the optics. We sat together in the furthest booth and drank Viennese coffee from tall white cups, served with water - an indulgence on my part, as caffeine is not good for the vocal cords. There was also a small glass dish of dark chocolate, broken into irregular pieces. I melted one on my tongue as he talked about the second Lieder:

Now I see well, why with such dark flames
in many glances you flash upon me
O Eyes: as if in one look
to draw all your strength together

The dark flames of loss - the excitement of approaching death, being alive in the face of death - he saw that in the music, and I had not. I had imagined all to be sadness, and had sung only that, removing all other colours from Mahler's palette.

'Death can be beautiful,' he told me, and I began to see it.

By the end of the evening, I will admit I asked him to come to my room with me. He had aroused me with his direct gaze, his way of speaking so openly on the darkest matters, and perhaps that is a terrible confession. Should one feel lust after discussing the death of children? Maybe only a lover of Mahler could understand it. For, yes, I came to Mahler that night, and Mozart always seemed a little too shiny for me afterwards.

In retrospect, it was perhaps a good thing that he declined my offer to accompany me upstairs. It would have made the evening less of a meeting of minds, and detracted from the many things he gave me to think about.

He kissed my cheek when he stood up to leave, talking of an early flight, and responsibilities at the hospital back home. The shock of his beard against my skin was delicious, and so sad; I felt sure we would never meet again.

'Thank you,' I said. 'I think you've made me a better singer.'

67

'So glad I could help. If you're ever in Pittsburgh...' He held out a business card. 'It was a delight to hear the Kindertotenlieder performed. It so very rarely is.'

'Yes. So many people think it's depressing.'

As I took the card, he caught my wrist and held it, for just a moment. 'But we know better.'

The sun always arises, radiant: those are the first lyrics. And they are right. By the end of that night and I was beyond the bad reviews and the silent audience. I had many more performances to give, and I vowed that every one would be better than the one before.

I read the card he had given me: Dr Adam Bexler. I took it with me to my room and slipped it inside the pages of my passport, in the small safe under the drinks cabinet. I kept it as a memento, nothing more. It travelled with me, across continents. After every success I held it in my hands and thought of him.

*

The next time I saw him was in New York.

Eight years had passed, and the Kindertotenlieder was in fashion for a change. Thousands had died when the planes flew into the towers. People had sons and daughters fighting overseas, in a war that felt without end. Death had come to America, and with my carefully timed CD release, I had become the voice of it.

The Met is a marvellous arena for a confident performer. The acoustics are wonderful; you can hear your voice soaring out over the tiers of seats, drowning out the rustling of programmes and the shifting of feet, which can be so distracting in a lesser venue. But I was not paying much attention to the auditorium that night; instead I was concentrating on the uncomfortable dress I had been persuaded to wear by my new costume manager. The diamante strappings around the chest were constricting my breathing, and I was finding it a battle to climb the peaks of the fourth Lieder:

They have just gone out ahead of us,
and will not be thinking of coming home.
We go to meet them on yonder heights
In the sunlight, the day is fine
On yonder heights.

I pictured firing my costume designer as soon as I got offstage; it was a diverting thought. I suppose I had become used to the vast, intense hush of the crowd that led to the wash of applause, breaking over me in waves, buoying me up from one performance to the next. In my defence, nobody seemed to care if the experience was true any more; they wanted to hear a famous singer, so that they could go home and tell their friends. How I sang no longer mattered.

And then I knew he was there.

It's difficult to describe how I became aware of him. It would have been impossible to pick out his features in that sea of faces, and yet I was utterly sure that he was attending that night, in the middle of the second tier. The connection between us was a thin thread of emotion, like a strand of silk, so delicate, so strong. Something in me came to life. Once more I felt the touch of his hand, the rough drag of his beard across my cheek. The constriction of my dress was forgotten. Instead I remembered what he had told me that night in Vienna, and I found passion within me, and projected it out to him with all of my skill. I sang only for him. I prayed that he did not find it wanting.

I sat in my dressing room for hours, after the final encore. He did not come.

There was a large square mirror, lit with old-fashioned bulbs, over the ornate dressing table. I don't know if it's still there now. It was the kind of mirror from which a performer could hide nothing.

That evening I saw the beginning of age on my face. Age is not in the appearance of fine wrinkles around the eyes, or a pouch of saggy skin forming under the chin. It is in experience: the darkness that creeps into the soul with every disappointment, lost love, broken promise. The soft child that lived inside me started to harden that night, as the minutes passed and I realised he was not coming to tell me I had pleased him. I had not done justice to Mahler yet again.

It hurt, the hardening of the child inside me; it hurt for many months, and I did not sing Mahler again for years. When I returned to the Kindertotenlieder and recorded it on CD for the first time another seven years had passed, and in that time I had been married and divorced, and lost both my parents. I was not the same woman any more. But I didn't realise how different I had become until I saw him for the last time.

*

He came into the reception, checking his watch, and the nurse at the main desk pointed him in my direction. I stood up, cardboard coffee cup in hand. I can recall his exact expression when he recognised me; it was the face a child pulls when a balloon pops at a birthday party – a mixture of instantaneous shock and glee that something so unexpected can happen, for no reason at all, and suddenly the world seems a little less controlled.

He set his lips together and walked towards me, both hands outstretched. I threw my coffee cup in the bin next to the dispenser and let him grasp my upper arms through my thick coat.

'I'm overwhelmed,' he said. 'What an honour.'

'So you remember me? It's been so many years.'

'I have your latest CD. My – er – wife bought it for me as a Christmas present.' He dropped his hands.

'And you still have your beard,' I said.

He stroked it. 'A little greyer.'

I became aware of the attention of the nurse, watching us as she languidly flipped through a file at the main desk. This was not how I'd imagined our meeting. I had constructed a scenario – a simple white room in which we came together and I had the time and space to ask the question that had haunted me since the release of the CD. But there was only here and now, in a small waiting room filled with plastic chairs, with the smell of the hospital and the sound

70

of footsteps and low conversations pressing around me. Still, I had to ask. There was no alternative, and time was already slipping away.

'Did I do it justice?' I said.

He seemed not to hear. 'Are you in Pittsburgh on – holiday?' Words were not coming easily to either of us.

'I came to see you. I still have your card.' I wanted to get it over with, now I'd started. 'I flew out from London, then caught a connecting flight from JFK. I phoned, of course, and they told me you still worked here. I spoke to a receptionist, or something. They said they'd put me through to your office and I realised I needed to see you in person. I can't explain it – I needed to know how you really felt about it.'

'The CD?' he said, slowly.

'It's crazy.' I could suddenly see it as if from a great distance - the ridiculousness of it. Maybe he had lost his love of Mahler. I could imagine him on his sofa, sitting next to his wife, reading a newspaper or surfing the web while the stereo bleated out soft, modern music. The three minute pop song ruled the world now, each note as bland and smooth as a boiled egg. Could that be his choice? But no, he had said he owned the CD. I could hope he had liked it.

The nurse came up, and said, 'Doctor Bexler, you asked me to remind you to check in on room 317 before your shift ended.'

'Yes, thank you.' For the first time he sounded like a doctor, dismissing a junior member of staff, too busy for conversations such as these.

'I should have handled this differently,' I said to him, as the nurse walked away.

He bit his lip, then said, 'Come with me.'

'Come –?'

'To room 317.'

I followed him, past the main desk. He keyed in a code and the secure door opened; he held it open for me and then steered me, one hand on my back, down a long corridor that the children had painted with flowers, stick figures, and an enormous yellow sun. The paint had been applied so thickly in places that it had dripped down the wall. It was impossible not to regard this bright messiness as a retort to the illnesses they faced. Or maybe the children who had made this mural had already lost their battle, and their flowers and faces meant nothing any more.

'Here,' he said, and a glass door on our left opened automatically. He ushered me in, and I found myself in a darkened room, filled with instruments and screens, all showing steady red or blue lights, and in the centre of them all was a girl on a bed, curled up in a ball, a tangled white sheet caught up under her arms and between her legs. She was bald, and tiny; she jerked in her sleep. From one arm ran a thin tube to a machine close to the bed, and on the other arm was a line to a drip, hanging above her, filled with a clear liquid.

He leaned in close to my ear. 'Liver cancer,' he whispered. I nodded. But it was too much to take in, this real death, the kind of illness he dealt with every day. I understood only that I had still failed to put this into my singing. The Kindertotenlieder still evaded me. I had no ability to show this dark room and the small, twitching body through the power of my voice.

'Watch,' he said. He stepped away from me, to the machine next to the girl's bed. He opened the outer panel on one side and pressed some buttons, quickly, lightly. I found myself watching the girl's face. She was not an angel, and there was nothing pure about her suffering. She was a bundle of flesh trying to curl in on itself, to make herself so small that pain would not be able to find her. She was a soldier at war, and I was watching her fight, even in her dreams.

He gestured for me to approach. I came up beside him as softly as I could, so as not to wake her, and put one hand on the edge of the bed, above the crumpled sheet. I wanted to ask him if she would win her struggle, but I didn't dare.

He held out his hand to me. In his fist he gripped a white wand, with a button set into the top. At first I thought it was a call buzzer for assistance, but when he pressed it no sound emanated. He kept his thumb down, and the girl stopped twitching. Her mouth fell open. Her body uncurled, became limp. I saw the fight leave her. I didn't understand. Not until it was too late, and he had set down the wand on top of the machine. Then he spoke, and this time he did not whisper.

'You see?' he said. 'You see how it is?'

And I did see.

'When they go, the very young ones, they become still, don't they? They leave the storm behind. As Mahler tells us. *They are resting, no more storms to be feared: by God's hand they are sheltered.*' He put both hands up to me, held them out as if presenting a gift. 'Or by my hands.'

I agreed with him; he had indeed brought shelter from the storm to that girl. And now she was as cold and pure as an angel, as a work of art, as a symphony.

I asked him if we could leave. I told him I had much to think about. He nodded, as if he understood, and escorted me back to the reception.

'I look forward to your next performance of the Kindertotenlieder,' he said, and kissed me on both cheeks. 'You can be sure I will attend.'

'Yes,' I said. 'Thank you.'

I went down to the lobby and summoned a taxi to take me to the police station.

*

And now I do not sing. Not even in the shower, or under my breath. I am afraid that I will find a phrase on my tongue, a moment of the Kindertotenlieder, and he will somehow hear it. Even though he will never tend to another child. He will no longer lead them through the storm to shelter before they are ready to give up their fight. Even though he is in prison, and I saw him sentenced, and taken away, for the deaths of so many children, over so many years.

If I sing, it will be there in my voice; the understanding of what it is to watch the death of a child. And so I will not sing again. And I will never have a child of my own.

73

Because there are some battles that one should not have to fight.

PENELOPE NAPOLITANO AND THE BUTTERFLIES

You can travel the world, you can see Kuala Lumpur and the Cote D'Azur, go everywhere, try anything; but it all comes down to one moment where you realise you're about to get engaged to a deeply lovely man who is undoubtedly going to turn you into your mother.

I'm only against turning into my mother on principle. She's a lovely woman, with a habit of phoning my mobile at inappropriate moments, say, in the middle of my snowboarding session. She likes digestive biscuits and fairy tales. She lives in Berkshire; has done all her life.

'Yes,' I shout, over the noise of the burners, 'Yes, I'll marry you.'

Tim's glorious smile, the one that I fell in love with, spreads to his ears, and over the faces of the other couple and the driver. Is driver the right word? Steerist, then. Airman. The man with his hand on the valve that makes this hot air balloon ascend, that's who I'm looking at, with his amused, patient expression that means *I've seen this all before.* Maybe he doesn't even believe in love anymore, with all the upping and downing he's done, and so many popped questions and champagne corks. He's probably thinking, as he bends down to flip open the lid of the coolbox, that he'd never marry a person who asked that kind of death-defyingly important question in public, with onlookers. That's what I always thought, until this moment. I'm having to revise my opinion of myself.

He produces a bottle of Bollinger and four plastic glasses. 'Congratulations!' shout the other couple, and the champagne is poured.

I shout, 'Thanks, wow, thanks, amazing,' and I can't take in the view, the soaring, razored peaks of the Rockies, because I have to drink and smile at these total strangers with expensive ski-jackets and messy, hot-air-balloon hair. That's suddenly become more important to me, making a good show. I'm my mother already.

Happy? mouths Tim.

The driver/airman/balloonist guy pulls a cord and turns a knob, and the burners diminish. We hang, for a weightless moment, and then begin to sink.

When I was little, sitting on the number 54 bus to Reading town centre, my mother would tell me stories about far-off places, and I used to ask her if they were real. I couldn't believe that there wasn't a kernel of truth in her tales of magic carpets and pirate galleons. There was one about a boy who lived on an island, a paradise, and he couldn't whistle. All he wanted was to be able to whistle. Such a small thing, and he couldn't do it; why did he make himself so miserable? My seven year old self couldn't understand it. Why reach for that which is beyond you? Why refuse to see the beauty of what is right in front of you?

Tim is gripping his plastic champagne glass in his enormous green ski-gloves. He's wearing a white strip of sunblock on the bridge of his nose, and he hasn't shaved for a few days, giving him a dusting of desirable stubble, and the appearance of a wild adventurer. I've known him for nine months; he's on secondment from an insurance company in Slough. Three more months and he expects to go home.

With me.

Can't real love be unsure? Can't it be delicate, wavering, affected by strong breezes? Must true love be like the mountains, so solid against all doubts?

There's a big orange butterfly sitting on the wicker basket.

With the burners turned down, I can hear the *Oooooh!* sounds of the other couple.

'It's a Monarch,' says the driver.

One of my mother's stories comes back to me. We're on the bus, heading back from shopping on a Saturday afternoon.

There's a big orange butterfly, the King of butterflies, and some tribes believe that if you capture it and whisper a wish to it, it will hold that wish for you because it has no choice but to be silent. But if you then let it go, in gratitude it will grant your wish.

I ask her, as we passed the trading estate – is that true?

No, Penelope, she says. *It's all pretend.*

Back in this life, I reach out, very slowly, and take the butterfly in my hands. I lift it to my lips and whisper to it. I can feel it listening.

Look! Says Tim. He's pointing to a squall on the horizon, a twisting orange cloud, moving fast, shimmering, falling over itself to reach us, and then a million Monarch butterflies are in my mouth and hair and hands, and I can hear their wings beating against the balloon, a sudden thunderstorm, deafening. They surround me, take me up on their wings; I feel them, like a hammock, and then there's no longer a basket, a balloon, a solid fiancé. There's only the air and the butterflies, taking me away, granting a wish for which I had no hopes.

Some of my mother's stories might be true after all.

*

I am borne away on the butterflies. I am ticklish to the touch of their wings; even though they are silent, I can't help laughing. I don't see much of the view as I giggle my way around the Rockies. Occasionally the ball of orange wings and black legs parts to form a window of sky or a glimpse of a clean white mountain: Grey's Peak, perhaps, or Mount Evans. I don't know. Colorado is beneath me, spread out like a map with no markers. Time is marked to the beat of insects.

Of course, eventually, I get hungry and thirsty. The fun aspect of the adventure begins to wear off.

'I want to get down,' I whisper to the butterflies, and then I amend that sentiment to, 'I'd like to be put down safely. Please. If

77

it's not too much trouble.' I don't feel a change in their course, and for a minute I have scary thoughts of staying up here in their ball of movement forever until I'm a skeleton, a ghost, only a strange memory in Tim's mind. But then I'd lifted upright on their wings and I feel my hiking shoes touch something solid.

The orange cloud shrinks away from me and disperses. I'm standing on the side of a freeway, next to a turnoff for a diner, the dated neon sign barely blinking in the strong sunlight. The Rockies are only a backdrop; this road is long and straight and without incline. There's nobody in sight. It's not a desert – the ground is lush, grassy, and there's a feeling of dampness to the warm air.

It takes a few attempts at walking before my legs start moving properly. I wobble up to the diner. It's one of those flat shiny buildings that Americans seem to like, and when I push open the door I feel I've walked into the set of a movie. There are red leather booths on my right and circular stools, the kind that spin, on my left, in front of a long counter with hot plates and a coffee machine that makes a reassuring plopping sound every now and again. The smell of bacon makes my stomach rumble. I make it to one of the booths.

While waiting for someone to serve me, I try to comb my fingers through my hair, but it's one gigantic knot, as if I've just driven at 150mph in an open-top convertible. Which, I suppose, I have.

I hear a door slam, and the sloppy clip-clop of high heels on vinyl flooring. A woman walks in from the open doorway behind the counter that I assume leads to the kitchen. She's wearing an orange dress with a black name tag, and a white Alice band in her black hair. She clocks me, and her eyes widen. She clip-clops over, biting her lips, pulling out a small pad and pencil from her breast pocket.

'Hello,' I say.

'Hey. What can I get ya?'

'Coffee and a bacon sandwich please. And I'm betting you have pie, right? Lots of pie. Do you have apple pie?'

'Sure thing, hon,' she says, with good humour. She is just what every American waitress should be.

78

'Do you have a map or something I could borrow?'

She tilts her head as she writes on the pad. 'Not much call for that around here.'

'For maps?'

'It's not like you get to have a say in where you're going, so, why take the time to look it up? I'll bring your coffee right over, just sit tight, hon.' She gives me a reassuring smile that has the opposite effect. Why am I getting no say? And how come a million butterflies flew me here? When I begin to actually think about it, it becomes obvious that I've gone crazy and probably jumped out of a hot air balloon in order to escape commitment and this is a moment of death dream type thing, so I hyperventilate for a while, and hit my head on the table a few times in the hope I'll wake up and find myself still alive. If that makes sense.

When the waitress brings over my coffee, she also brings a brown paper bag. 'Breathe into that, hon.' She holds it to my lips and eventually I stop trying to suck up all the air in the world all at once. 'Don't fight it so hard, okay? You're not crazy and you're not dead. You're flying Monarch, hon. Relax and enjoy it.'

'Pardon?'

'The Butterfly Express Route? To Happiness? That's what you wished for, right?'

'Not exactly.' I sip the coffee. It's delicious. 'I wished for...' What did I wish for? And why would a butterfly take me seriously?

'You wished for some kinda answer. To everything. To why you are the way you are, and where you're meant to be.'

I look up at her, her wiry black hair and the orange dress. 'This is the weirdest dream ever.'

'Hang on in there, hon. I'll get your bacon.' She pats me on the arm and clip-clops back to the kitchen.

I hear, from nowhere, the theme tune to *The Muppet Show*.

Wait; it's not from nowhere. It's from the inner pocket of my ski jacket. It's my mobile phone. I unzip the jacket and dig out my phone. The display says – Mum.

'Hello?'

'Hello Pennie, love, have I caught you at a bad moment?'

'No, it's perfect timing,' I tell her. 'Listen, I'm, I'm at this place, this diner, and it's like...'

'Are you having some dinner? What time is it over there? I was worried you'd be in bed.'

'Why? What time is it?' It's broad daylight outside, but suddenly I'm suspicious of it, of time and place and the entire universe and my assumptions about it. 'Are you okay, mum? Have you seen any butterflies?'

'Butterflies? It's October.'

'Listen, don't worry about me, okay? No matter what you hear, I'm okay.'

'Okay,' she says, her voice peppered with suspicion.

'Some stories are true after all.'

'Well,' she says. There's a pause. 'I would have thought you'd have worked that out by now. And some truths we all rely on have never been true at all.'

I can't begin to deal with that concept. 'What do you mean?'

'Pennie?'

'Yeah.'

'I don't like digestive biscuits.'

My bacon sandwich arrives. My waitress puts the orange-rimmed plate down on the table and winks, and the phone goes dead. 'Better eat up,' she says. 'Restroom's out back if you need it. Your ride leaves in five.'

*

We get down to Mexico in no time at all. Or, at least, with no helpful sign of time passing: no sunrises, no nights, and no desire to be either awake or asleep. I drift along, stopping occasionally for steak and eggs or blueberry pancakes, and my mobile stays surprisingly silent. I think about phoning my mother back and continuing our conversation about digestive biscuits but I don't want to find out more. What did she mean, that she never liked them? Then why has she always eaten two of them with a small cup of tea after dinner? Why does she put them in the shopping trolley every week? The thought that she has eaten digestives against her will for decades bothers me more than the fact that I'm being carried to a new country on a cloud of butterflies

I think about Tim, too. He's always in my mind.

I know we're in Mexico because there's a sombrero obscuring the neon sign and the waitress in the orange dress has adopted a terrible fake accent.

'Eh, gringo,' she says, 'You want the tacos?'

'Whatever.'

'They are the best in all Mehico.'

'I don't doubt it.' I plonk myself down in the booth, and she drops the accent.

'What's up?'

'I don't know where we're going. I don't know what I'm doing. It's been one hell of a ride, but, seriously, Mexico? What's in Mexico?'

'The spawning grounds,' she says, as if that was painfully obvious. 'The Butterfly Biosphere reserve, on the border of Michoacan. Every October the butterflies travel, millions of them, to that one place. And there, everything becomes still. They sit on the trees. Peace reigns. It's a moment of inner contentment that few are blessed with. Trust me, things will become clear to you there. Things that weren't clear before. Like whether you should get married and why your mother never liked digestive biscuits.'

'Oh,' I say. 'Right. In that case, I'll have the tacos.'

She nods, puts away her notepad, and clip-clops back to the kitchen.

Given that such an amazing life experience awaits me at The Biosphere, I feel surprisingly calm. I think all emotion is leaving me; I'm emptying out my fear, my pain, my excitement and my happiness. Even my feelings for Tim no longer seem real. They've been chased away by the flapping of a million orange wings.

When the tacos arrive I can't even appreciate their spiciness. My tongue is as dead as my heart.

81

*

It's midnight at The Biosphere. The moon is enormous, full to bursting. The butterflies cling to the black trees, spent, breathless. I lie in the grass, surrounded by the pillars of their exhaustion, a testament to their journey. Thousands of miles have been travelled.

I take my mobile from my pocket and dial home. My mother answers. I picture her, standing in the hall, next to the phone's cradle even though I bought her a cordless one last Christmas. She's never got used to the idea that she's free to move around.

'Digestive biscuits,' I say. It's the first thing that I think of.

'Pardon?'

'You don't like them.'

'No, not much.' She sighs. 'Are you sure you're ready for this story, love? Only you've never seemed very ready to hear anything real I had to say before. Particularly about your dad.'

'Yes,' I say. 'Maybe that's true. But I feel ready now. I'm in a different place.'

'Yes,' she agrees. 'You sound different.' The butterflies move their trembling wings to my heartbeats. 'I moved to Napoli. Three years before you were born. Your dad was homesick, and I said I would try living there. We moved in with his mother. You're very like her. She wasn't good at listening either. That's not always a bad thing, I mean, you know your own mind. I've never been so sure as you. About anything. But I knew I didn't like Napoli.'

'Why not?'

'There was nothing for me to hold on to, nothing familiar to anchor me. I felt so... up in the air.'

'But that can be a good thing!' I say. 'You've never been open to it. But to be free, to be weightless, it can be...'

'Can I tell you the rest?' my mother says. 'Please? Right. Your dad knew I was unhappy. He tried so hard to help me settle in. The only English food he could find in the market were packets of digestive biscuits; he brought them home from work with him every day, and I didn't have the heart to tell him I'd never really liked

82

them. His mother called them disgusting. She couldn't see what was wrong with the amaretti she made; she took it as a rejection. Which it was. I did reject her, and everything Italian. I didn't really try very hard. I can admit that now. I cried and cried. Eventually I persuaded your dad to give up his job and return to England with me. He was never really right, after that. He thought he'd let his mother down, somehow, and I didn't care enough about that to realise it would be the end of us. Just after you were born his mother had a stroke. He went back to Napoli to care for her, and after she died he never came back. I never asked him to come back, I suppose. Yes. I never once asked him to come back, and if you don't chase what you want, it doesn't happen.'

'Why didn't you ask him?' I say.

There is a silence. Then she says, 'So I keep buying the digestive biscuits because they remind me of him. And because I think I don't deserve to eat amaretti. His mother made the most wonderful amaretti.'

'So there was one thing about Napoli you liked.'

'Yes, love, I suppose there was.'

I say goodbye and put away my phone. I think about what she has told me, and why I would never had understood it before this moment. But I have been weightless, babied, on the wings of a dream. I know that it is not enough to be carried away to a new place. You have to know what to do when you get there.

I close my eyes and whistle a nameless tune. I think about the place to which Tim wants to take me. I can picture it clearly. There will not be butterflies, or hot air balloons. But there will be digestive biscuits. My mother is right; I'm not like her. I know my own mind, and I happen to quite like digestive biscuits.

When the butterflies are ready to return to Canada, maybe they will take me back to Tim. I'm going to give him a proper answer.

FORGET ME KNOT

'When your mother got married she wanted a bouquet of forget-me-nots,' Mr Treever said. 'The florist told her it couldn't be done. Those are wild flowers, not to be cultivated, and they die only an hour after they're picked. But your mother wouldn't have it. So your Grandad had to put her in the horse and carriage, all dressed in white with a veil that trailed on the floor, and ride around the countryside for hours until he found a patch of forget-me-nots. By the weir they were. He picked an armful, took her to the church, and pushed her down the aisle with his shotgun trained on her back.'

I pictured a forget-me-not in my head: a small, delicate flower, with soft petals and tiny leaves, a beautiful fragrance forever cradled in my mother's arms. 'What did she look like, Mr Treever?'

'Hugely fat. Like a magnificent white whale. And your father, eyes raised to the vaulted ceiling, tapping the ground expectantly although he must have felt the vibrations as she lolloped down the aisle towards him in that festooned marquee of a wedding dress. He had the grizzled, intent expression of an Ahab that day, with that impressive beard thrown over one shoulder. So they fitted together, you see, my angel. It was a marriage made in heaven, even if they had to be forced to do it. They preferred the raw passion of adultery, you see.'

Mr Treever had read *Moby Dick* to me over a month of evenings, so I understood his description a little more than usual. His words were always like puzzle boxes to me. Sometimes, when he left me alone in my room to sleep, I woke to realise my hands were scrabbling in my hair as if I could grab hold of the strange images he implanted in my mind and tease meaning from them.

The quick, even ticking on my left that kept me company was replaced by the tinkle of bright music, a little tune, four sounds repeated four times.

'Oil time,' I said. My favourite time.

84

'Yes, pet.' I heard my bedside drawer squeak open and slam shut. I could picture the bottle of oil in his hands: those long, thin fingers; the rough skin of his square palms.

'But they grew to love each other, didn't they? My mother and father?'

'I wouldn't say love,' Mr Treever mused. 'Not for each other. But they loved you very much, because you were so much like both of them.'

'My mother's size and my father's blindness,' I said. I felt my silk sheet slide from my body, down from my collarbones to my knees. A breeze from the open window on my right caught the hairs on my arms and legs and stirred them into erectness. The skin under my left breast itched. I slid my hand into the fold and scratched.

'Bad lass. You're making it red,' Mr Treever admonished.

'What's red?'

'Sore. Marked. Swollen. Inflamed. Dangerous.'

I pictured my dangerous breast, sucking blood from my vast body like a giant, pulsing parasite. I dropped my hand.

'Good girl.' And then there was a dripping of the oil, slow, deliberate, into my navel until it ran down the mountainside of my waist and soaked into the silk sheet beneath me. 'Oh dear,' Mr Treever said in his soft, slow voice. 'We'll have to change the bed later.'

I waited for the pressure of his hands. When they came there was pleasure, vast serene lakes of pleasure, and I sailed away on them like the giant, beautiful whale I was. 'Tell me about my father,' I sighed.

'He was a spy.'

'A brilliant spy.'

'An incredible spy, for who would think a blind man so capable? But intelligence and ingeniousness runs in your veins. He could climb the blank faces of tall buildings, speak twenty languages, hold his breath for four minutes, and his cane hid a knife as sharp as his wit. For emergencies only, that secret knife, you understand, and he only ever had to use it once. That was the time, the only time, he was captured.'

85

'When? Where?'

'You were yet to be born, I believe, and the honeymoon was in full swing on the remote island of Zanzibar, which is a mystical place of aromas and textures, birds and insects, when the enemy came for him and took him by surprise, lifting him from his bed without disturbing your sleeping mother. She awoke to find herself alone and assumed he had left her for one of the dark-skinned beauties of the island, as they all smelled of sunshine and citrus, two things your father couldn't resist. She came home alone, distraught, and could never really forgive him, even when she found out the truth. Doubt had entered her life, you see, duckling. Doubt destroys passion.'

I pictured doubt as a cloud of nibbling flies, landing on my mother's ears and eyes, crawling into her head and laying their eggs in the meaty creases of her mind. I shuddered at the thought.

'Are you cold, dear heart? Shall we stop?' I heard eagerness in his voice.

'Just a little longer. So what happened to my father? Where did the enemy take him?'

'A Siberian Gulag. All ice and snow and cold, with thin, ripped clothes and torture beyond endurance. But the physical punishment was nothing to a man like him. It was the mental tests that wore him down. Every day he was placed in a room with a puzzle to solve. It was as if they wanted to understand how his mind worked, so that they might try to make more men like him. They couldn't understand that he was a product of his own deficiency. He had grown around his blindness in new, amazing directions.'

My father. In my mind he had tubers of achievement springing from his long wiry beard, and his proud head raised high to spite his own blindness. 'What kind of puzzles?'

Mr Treever's hands rested on my thighs for a moment, then recommenced their rhythmic movements. 'Sometimes as simple as a jigsaw. Sometimes a shape to be made from paper or clay, or the next move on a chessboard. One time they demanded that he tattooed a tree on to the left buttock of a naked woman. He said she never once moved while he worked, and her skin was as cold as marble.

But she whispered to him constantly, in a strange language which he thought might be a form of Polynesian, a begging, desperate tone to her musical voice. When he finished the tattoo, they strangled her in front of him. He heard her last choked breaths, and knew at the moment that they had broken him. The next puzzle would be his last.'

The ticking on my left gave way to the chimes once more. I listened to the little tune by which my life was lived. Mr Treever's hands left my body. I heard the rustle of the silk sheet by my knees. 'Leave it,' I said, 'and tell me about the final puzzle.'

He sighed in assent. 'The next day, after a long night of beatings and electrocutions, he was taken to the room as usual and left alone to discover what trial awaited him. He crawled forward and discovered two objects: his cane, a small act of kindness designed to humiliate him, he surmised; and a small metallic object which he identified as a canister. But holding what? For what? Even the most basic of deductions eluded him. He sat down next to both objects and let time pass. He would play games no more.

'Time moved on. Your father grew nervous, despite his resolution not to care. Would they think the canister had defeated him? Would they kill him, or, worse, think less of him? As the hours slipped away, his resolve trembled and cracked. He had to pass the test. He could not let a simple canister defeat him.

'And so he picked it up and examined it.

'He ran his finger over the smooth metal, feeling for any kind of distortion on the surface. None was apparent. The distant sound of doors being opened had his heart racing, and he desperately twisted the metal object, but his efforts were futile. He cried in frustration, rocking on his knees as heavy footsteps echoed down the hall. The door was thrown back, and the bang against the prison wall was followed by the sound of laughter, raucous, mocking laughter from the mouth of the guard.

'Your father had failed. He failed, and he was a destroyed man.'

I pictured my father, shattered, falling into shards of glass on the cold floor of his cell, so sharp in defeat that my dead eyes were cut and bleeding from the thought, the liquid falling over my cheeks. Mr Treever dabbed at my face with his soft, sweet-smelling handkerchief. He spoke on, his voice low, close to my ear.

'But he was not beaten for long. He grabbed his cane, unsheathed his blade, and ran the guard through. Then he picked up the canister and carried it like a baby across the icy wasteland of Siberia, until he found your mother and freedom once more. You had been born by then, a blubbery ball of blind loveliness, and you replaced the canister in his arms. He kept it in the corner of your nursery, as if the two of you were somehow linked.

'They were so proud of you, and they remained devoted to your every need until the day they were killed by that enemy missile strike. Thank goodness you were with me that day, petal, and you've been with me every day since.'

'And do you love me, Mr Treever?' I asked.

'I adore you, angel. Now, can I pull up the sheet?'

I nodded my assent, and enjoyed the sensation of silk sliding easily over my oiled, undulating skin once more.

'Now, what would you like for your dinner?'

'Venison,' I said. 'A whole deer. With a wheel of blue cheese, and three heads of lettuce.'

'As you wish. And then I'll read to you. You're enjoying The Mayor of Casterbridge, aren't you?'

'Very much. And then you must change my sheets,' I said. A bird chirped outside my window. I imagined its song as an arc from its mouth to my bed, a pattern of beauty that flew apart and dissolved into death only a moment after it had been born.

'It's time,' I said. 'Give it to me.'

Mr Treever didn't speak. He knew better than to try to dissuade me. I heard the clunk of metal under the bed, and a moment later the canister was in my hands, cold and smooth, the puzzle that couldn't be solved. I touched it all over, shook it, repeated actions I had done a hundred times before.

'Get out,' I said to Mr Treever. 'Leave me in peace.'

'Of course.' I heard his feet shuffle away from me, then stop. 'Will you, maybe, duckling, give some thought to what we talked about before? About getting up, out of this room, seeing how you like real life?'

'Don't make me angry, Mr Treever,' I warned him, and he left.

I had to keep trying. One day the canister would have to give up its secret to me. It would bow to my will, my tremendous will, that bar of iron secreted within my folds of fat. And inside the canister would be something magnificent. I could picture it – a soft explosion of forget-me-nots, those tiny dots joined by twining, singing leaves and the smell of love upon them, sinking into my skin, making me as magnificent as my mother forever more.

Mr Treever would tell me the story again tomorrow. Every day I came closer to understanding.

MIDNIGHT
MIDNIGHT

I kiss his photo, like a line in a song, and put it back under the cash register.

The door is pushed open, and the small brass bell above it tinkles.

How quaint! says the woman, *I didn't expect that,* and *They've got Chakka, get a basket,* to the man who trails after her. He glances at me and I point to the stack of wire baskets next to the counter. He approaches with small steps, and wrestles one basket free; he has to tug hard. Then he returns to his lady and she stacks the Chakka into it, eight packets, the maximum allowed.

She rubs her hands on her skirt and wanders down the furthest aisle. I watch her on the monitor under the counter as she fingers the confectionery, then picks up some multicoloured sweets and pops them in the basket. She flips her hands at her man, a shooing gesture in my direction. His shoulders slumped, he returns to me. I can read fear in his fleshy, trembling mouth. I'm getting better at reading their expressions, although at first they all looked the same to me.

He puts the basket on the counter and I ring up the items.

Eighty-seven, I tell him, struggling with the s as usual, and he frowns, but takes out his wallet and produces his card. I reach for it, and he flinches, but stands his ground; I fumble it into the reader and a moment later the transaction is complete.

He links arms with his happy, hurrying woman, and they take their purchases home. They'll gorge on them tonight, as all first-timers do, and they'll feel sick and sorry tomorrow. But they'll come back for more, and become regulars, losing a little more of their fear of me every time they step into my shop, but none of their revulsion. Every person is the same. They hate me for giving them what they want.

I restock the shelf with Chakka.

*

It must be night out there. The packs of young men have descended, swaggering into the shop and asking for alcohol along with their Chakka. Sometimes they pick up crisps and instant meals as well; I keep a few of these local products for this kind of customer.

The leaders of these packs have become easy to pick out by their glare, their stance. This one has a small beard on a long chin. Facial hair fascinates me. It looks so itchy. When he puts both hands on my counter and leans in, I'm too busy thinking about that beard, and the waft of grain-based alcohol that comes out of his mouth, to hear what he says. I have to ask him to repeat himself.

Have you got any ciggies?

I turn around and sort through the shelves behind me; I hear him slip a packet of crisps into the pocket of his hooded top. When I turn back, cigarettes in hand, he is smirking at his three friends, who have come up behind him, holding handfuls of Chakka. I put the cigarettes on the counter and ring up everything, including the crisps. He doesn't notice. He's too busy staring at the cigarettes.

What's the fuck's these?

It's too difficult to explain that it's a chemically produced tobacco derivative, complete with nicotine, apricot extract, and Akan-I, one of the relaxants found in Chakka. Instead I shrug, and say, *That's all we've got.*

Fucking hell, he says.

You want it?

Yeah, yeah, how much?

Hundred and fifty two, I tell him, expecting him to make a scene, and he doesn't disappoint me.

How much? You fucking money-grabbers, coming here, putting people out of jobs, selling your shit, you fucking ugly little yellow baldie, out for all you can get...

His friends put their hands on him, and pull him back from the counter. One of them produces a card. *Here, put it on this, all right? He don't mean nothing. He's just had a few, that's all.*

I complete the transaction and return the card. Just another swipe at what should be the end of a long day. But this isn't a long day; it is the endless day. And I am lost in it, like my lover, so many millions of miles away. As I am left alone again, I permit myself to take out his photo and stroke the lines of his face with my claws. Studying his expression at that moment, when I turned the camera upon him and said smile! It takes up so much of my time. When we are together again I will have become an excellent judge of what every grimace and grin means.

Fascinating faces. Everyone has such a fascinating face.

*

Remembrance of Things Past, says the cracked spine of the book. She's a little over half way through, and getting slower every day. Today she's only pretending to read, I can tell from the way she holds the book low so she can glance over the top at me, so I call to her –

You want tea?

Yes please, she says. I heat up two instant teas in the microwave and take them over to her, balancing the tray on the backs of my hands. She is sitting on a rung of the ladder that leads up to the top shelves, where the electronics are kept. She puts the book down on the floor and takes the tea, sipping it, wrinkling up her face. It's an old face, with deep folds in the papery skin. I find the older faces easier to look at. Less shiny.

It's very kind of you, she says. She never had any real fear of me, not even when she first came in to the shop and asked me if it was true that time stopped inside it. Then she asked if she could stay, just for a little while every day, in order to finish her book. Her fear of her tumour blotted out her fear of me. Her fear of not getting to finish the book.

You shouldn't break the rules for me, she says.

It's okay.

If I'm caught letting her stay, they'll never let me come home again. But how would they find out? They're all so far away. When I get back home, and time restarts for me and my love, we'll be rich and happy and still young. Although it occurs to me now that maybe being young isn't to do with what age you are, but what you saw in the time that passed.

I don't know why, but I fetch the photo from under the till and show it to her. She looks at it with interest, craning her neck, and she says, *how lovely, is that a relative?*

My... I touch my chest. Surely she will understand that; our hearts are all in the same place.

Your other half? Lovely. You must miss him.

When the Chakka is gone, I can go home. And the same for him. Then we can be together.

Is that going to take a long time?

The back room of the shop is filled with Chakka. The back room does not obey the laws of space, just as the front does not obey the laws of time. I don't know how long it will take to empty that room, but at least I know humans will want to buy as much as I can sell.

No time here, I tell her. *No day, no night, no sleeping, no waking up.*

No, she says, that's right. *You never close, do you? When I was young we used to have seven elevens. I suppose that makes you a midnight midnight. I don't know how you do it.*

No, I say. *But it's okay.*

There are many things I'd like to say to this woman, for whom time moves far too quickly. But she is thinking about something else. When she does this her eyes slide away and she purses her lips, and I know she is not listening any more. I take my photo back to the counter.

And she puts down her tea, and returns to her book.

*

It must be morning, for the business people are arriving, and the shop is filled with them, picking up their newspapers and croissants and, of course, their supply of Chakka for the day. There is a river of cards to be swiped; it dries up to a trickle, and the rush is over. The same will happen later, in reverse, as they return from work.

The shop is empty apart from one man, in a suit. He is sweating; I can smell it. He approaches the counter with armfuls of Chakka, more than is legally allowed for one purchase. I look into his face and see desperation.

I'll pay for it, he says. *I need it for my family.*

No.

My mum and dad aren't well, they can't get down here, I need all this for them, they've asked me to get it for them.

No. No, I tell him, and I see the moment he decides to take it. He turns for the door, and I jump over the counter and reach for him, my claws extended. As usual, I've miscalculated the pressure; my claws puncture his suit and sink into his body, and he arches his back, then slumps forward. I try to remove my claws and rip holes in him. The material comes away, and he oozes. I use my other hand to decapitate him, to put him out of his misery. Then I pick up his head and his body and move them to the back room.

The Chakka he was trying to take is spoiled. I have to throw that away too. And I clean the floor, with a packet of wipes I keep under the counter for these incidents.

His face, frozen, as I held his head in my hands, was not of fear, but of surprise, as if he hadn't expected this to happen. And yet, he had to know the risks. But we tell ourselves, no matter where we come from and what we look like, that we are somehow immune to the dangers of the paths we choose to take.

I hope I will see my beloved again, and we will be young again, and happy. I hope that we will be some of the lucky shopkeepers that survive the attentions of our customers. But I know that one night they will come with a plan to take the Chakka, and I will not be fast enough to deal with them all.

I wonder what their faces will look like. If I study them hard enough, maybe I will be able to read their intentions in their expressions, and I will have gained an advantage. Maybe enough of an advantage to keep me alive.

After I've finished cleaning up, I retreat to the counter and take out my photo. I stare at it until the next customer comes.

CATERPILLAR

At first, it whistled. Early in the pregnancy, while Kate was still suffering from morning sickness, she kept catching a sound behind her, and turning, thinking the kettle was boiling or someone was trying to attract her attention. It took her over a month to work out that it was coming from inside her.

Then it would laugh, particularly first thing in the morning when it took her a minute to struggle up from the mattress and longer to pull her clothes on. She thought maybe it had the hiccups – she had heard her cousin talk about her baby having hiccups in the womb – but it only happened when Kate was frustrated by her growing size, or in pain. It seemed the baby found her suffering funny.

She waited a long time before she told Greg, knowing what he would say. But she had to talk to someone about it, so for a whole week she let him have the remote control to himself and didn't complain when he talked about getting a motorbike in the hope that when she raised the subject on Sunday evening, in the lull of The Antiques Roadshow, he wouldn't give her that look.

Her feet were on his lap, and he was watching a chest of drawers get valued as he rubbed them.

'Greg, the baby laughs,' she said.

'Isn't he a bit young for that yet?' Greg said. 'Can you believe that piece of junk was worth eight grand? I could do with some of that. Could get myself a Triumph. And something nice for the baby.'

'Well, it was whistling too. But now it laughs.'

He took her feet from his lap and stood up. 'Want a cup of fruit tea?'

'No, thanks. I want to talk to you about the baby.'

'Babies can't whistle, love. There's no air in there. It must be trapped wind.'

'I know the difference between whistling and trapped wind!'

He switched off the television and gave her that look. 'Well, you're going through a lot of changes, and you can't expect to know what's happening in there. Make an appointment with the doctor—he'll put your mind at rest. I'll make you a fruit tea.'

He wandered off in the direction of the kitchen.

It was the first time someone had suggested to her that she should no longer expect to know anything about herself. Any emotion, pain, feeling or intuition could now be assigned to the pregnancy – it was in control of her, and Greg and the doctors were in control of it.

The next morning she started talking back to the baby.

When she tried to pick up the newspaper from the living room floor and strained her back, it gave a little giggle. She heard it.

'Show some respect to your mother,' she said, 'or I'll give you what for.'

The giggling stopped. Instead, from inside her, there emanated a wary silence.

'There,' she said. 'That's better.'

So, for a while, it appeared that it was just a case of needing to be the boss.

About a month later, six months into the pregnancy, it upped the stakes. It spoke to her.

Kate was struggling to rub some moisturising cream into her lumpy thighs. Standing naked in front of the bedroom mirror, she reminded herself of a gigantic white, blue-veined caterpillar, twisting around, bulging with the potential to split open and reproduce. All that would be left of her after the birth was a pile of skin on the floor. The baby was draining her of life.

'That's right,' it said.

She stopped rubbing her thighs.

'Gonna change you,' it said. 'Heh.'

Kate dragged herself to the edge of the bed and sat down. The springs crunched under her weight.

'Moron,' it said.

'Stop insulting me,' she whispered.

'I've got your number. I know all about you. You've got no idea, have you?'

'Shut up,' she said, trying to shout, but her voice was barely louder than the one inside her. She lay down and jammed a pillow over her head. 'Shut up.'

'Don't you know you've got me forever? Might as well get used to it.'

'No…'

'Shall I open your eyes, metaphorically speaking?'

Kate threw the pillow across the room and jammed her fingers in her ears.

'You are funny,' the voice said fondly. 'Funny Mummy. I know something you don't know. You're little better than a baby yourself, doing what you're told, listening to the experts. If you can listen to them, you can listen to me. And I've got plenty to say. Let's start with self-knowledge, shall we? Every human being has the ability…'

It took an eternity for the clock to crawl round to five, and another twenty minutes for Greg to get home from work.

'Talk to it,' she demanded, pointing at her stomach.

Greg pulled off his coat and hung it on the rack. 'Nice to see you too,' he said. 'I could do with a coffee and kiss hello.'

'Tell it to stop.'

He kneeled down and put his lips against her bump. 'Stop being mean to Mummy, tiger,' he whispered, and then looked up at her, smiling. 'How was that?'

'Crap,' the voice inside her said. 'Did you really think that would work?'

She stomped off into the kitchen and switched on the kettle. A moment later, she felt Greg's hands push between her arms to stroke her stomach. 'What's up?'

'You wouldn't believe me,' she said. 'Just do me a favour and stay out of my way for a while. Go and look at bikes on the computer.'

'Is he being bad in there?' He tapped a spot just below her belly button, and the baby moved in response.

She slapped his hands away. 'Get off me!'

'Fine.'

Greg left the kitchen. Kate refused to act on her impulse to go after him.

'He's not very masterful, is he?' the voice inside her said. 'Bit of a loser, actually.'

'I'm beginning to realise that,' she muttered.

'So you're finally getting the idea! You have to take responsibility for this yourself. It's no good expecting a man to save you. Let me tell you about personal freedom and how to fight for it…'

'Please don't,' she begged, but it had already launched into another speech.

*

The next three months felt like a lifetime to Kate.

When she finally went into labour, one cold Thursday morning, she phoned Greg at work to come and pick her up. She couldn't stop crying all the way to the hospital. There was no way she could explain to Greg that she was crying with relief.

'You've got at least another five hours to go, dear,' the midwife said. 'It's too early to be pushing.'

'Are you going to let someone else dictate to you about your body?' the voice in Kate said.

'It's coming now!' she screamed.

'Listen to the midwife,' Greg urged.

'He really is totally ineffectual,' the voice said. 'Tell him to piss off.'

'Piss off!' she shouted into Greg's face. He retreated to the far end of the room and pushed open the curtain to look outside.

'That wasn't nice,' the midwife told her, wagging her finger.

The voice inside Kate came up with a few choice descriptions for the midwife, and she passed them all on. The midwife backed out of the room and a minute later the doctor arrived.

'Hello,' he said. 'Shall I take a look?'

He peered between her legs.

'Pervert,' the voice inside Kate said. 'You know he's getting a thrill out of this? A man seeing a woman in pain. It makes his day.'

'Oh,' the doctor said. 'The baby's coming now.'

'We told you that!' the voice and Kate said simultaneously, and then the pushing began, drowning out all other considerations.

*

Kate looked down into the face of her newborn daughter.

Her daughter didn't look back at her. Her eyes were shut, and her face was empty. She was a blank slate. She had no ideas of her own yet.

She had no voice.

'Did you really think my voice was coming out of a baby?' something inside her said.

*

'You're not doing it right,' Kate said to Greg, snatching the nappy away from him. 'I'll do it. Can't you ever get anything right?'

'Sorry,' Greg said, moving to one side. He pulled a face at the baby. She was too young to smile, but Greg thought he could see happiness shining out of her little face. 'She's going to be a stunner when she grows up, isn't she?'

'Don't put your unimportant assumptions on our child, Greg. It's not what she looks like, it what she thinks that matters.'

'Sorry,' Greg said again. He couldn't seem to say it enough nowadays. He got up and slouched into the computer room, hoping to look at a few bikes before Kate used the opportunity to tell him he was being brainwashed, wanting the thrill of speed as a macho bullshit statement.

Motherhood had altered her, no doubt about it. All his friends had said the same thing – they change once they get pregnant.

Suddenly you're not important any more. Only the baby matters. Nothing pleased Kate any more, and when he tried to ask her what was wrong, she told him that he couldn't possibly understand.

He understood one thing – he understood mothers and daughters. Kate used to moan about her own mother, saying she was a battleaxe, too demanding, refusing to accept what Kate wanted out of life, saying Greg was never good enough, her life was never good enough.

Give it fifteen years, and his daughter would be saying the same thing about Kate. And he'd be tempted to agree with her.

Greg looked at a picture of a Triumph and imagined freedom.

FOR ROSEBUD

A broken streetlight.

It blinked on, and the crowding brick walls and pavement took on a rain-wet glow. It blinked off, and the night swallowed the street.

It blinked on.

Beneath it, a dirty pool had formed around the grate of the drain. A sheet of newspaper lay trapped in the bars. It unfolded, surrendering to the swell, and its headline was tugged into view.

Invasion Imminent

The doorway to the nearby hotel was in shadow, covered by the striped awning that kept it dry. It would have been easy to think it was an empty space, except for something shiny, at floor level: two patent leather toecaps, side by side, curved like convex lenses. The raindrops bounced on them.

The streetlight blinked off, and the pebbles disappeared. The rain intensified, and time hung unmoving, like the lights glowering over an emptied London.

It blinked on. The toecaps had moved a few inches apart, and one was half-covered by a curtain of black material: a trouser leg. A bald head jerked into the light, as bright as the moon and covered with as many craters. The pockmarks, some small, some large, spread down over the face of the man who looked old but well-kept: his grey eyebrows were groomed; his face was freshly shaved; and the Windsor knot in his tie was pulled up tight under the folds of his hangdog neck.

He pulled a phone, snug and smooth, from the pocket of his raincoat. He flipped it open and pressed the keypad.

'Rosebud,' he said. 'I'm going to meet him now. Keep safe.'

The light blinked off. Footsteps sounded like cymbals in the percussion of raindrops.

The light blinked on to a deserted street. The sheet of newspaper swirled in circles. Then it gave itself over to the pull of the drain, and was gone.

*

'Chicken pox,' Kane said. 'When I was a kid. Never thought I'd had it bad when I had hair. Then I got older, started losing the hair, and so I shaved it off – found these pockmarks underneath. Scared the shit out of my wife. View's incredible up here.'

He took one hand from his sopping raincoat and gestured at London, laid out beneath him like a butterfly under glass, dead and fragile and beautiful, all at the same time. Then he stared up, through the roof of the capsule, at the night sky and the clusters of kaleidoscopic lights that had become visible the day before yesterday. He hadn't made a decision as to what he thought about them yet. Blind panic had taken everybody else on the planet and somehow passed him by.

'Is she used to it now?' Staff said.

Kane turned to him, still squinting from the lights, and quirked his lips to show he wasn't offended by the question. 'She's dead. And no, she never did get used to it. Who would have ever thought this would be the safest place to meet?'

'It was easy to get going. The control booth was open. You'd have thought the last one out of London would have padlocked the Eye. Obviously not on the list of priorities.' He laughed, and the fluid motion of the tilt of his head accentuated his youth, and his fear. He was handsome in a boyish way, Kane thought. If this was the end, Staff had been robbed of a good ten years of easy lays before the lifestyle of debauchery took its toll. Kane felt sorry for him.

'Don't be afraid,' Kane said on impulse, and Staff flinched, as if a scab had been knocked from a wound. 'At least, not of me. I still want to do the deal.'

Staff nodded. He was dressed all in black, as if attending a costume ball as a secret agent. He bit his lip as he held out the large rectangular case he carried by its fraying brown strap. 'Okay, then let's trade.'

'Got some other place to be?'

'What's it to you?'

'I could use some company, that's all. What say we do this the old-fashioned way – have a conversation. Pass the time of day.' He gestured at the view, and couldn't help saying, 'Watch the world go round. For a while.'

'I don't do chit-chat,' Staff said, and Kane almost laughed at his fake swagger. He managed to turn it into an indulgent smile instead.

'Try.'

'So what did your wife die of?'

Kane sat on the thin white bench and felt the movement of the capsule through his thighs. 'TB. Six months ago.'

'Oh, right. Sorry.'

'That's okay,' he said easily. He had become used to discussing it without allowing the still fresh emotions to surface; he simply didn't picture Bella as he said it. He felt less guilty about that than remembering her as an antibiotic-pumped shell.

'Perhaps its better she went rather than live to see this.' Staff gestured at the lights above and the black, empty buildings below.

'That's the kind of thing only the very young say,' Kane said. He hadn't meant it as an insult, but Staff seemed to take it that way. His shoulders tightened. He was out of his depth, involved in a deal he didn't understand. It explained the nerves, the bravado. 'You know, in all the books about this sort of thing, mankind bands together. They forget their differences. Look for a common solution. Why do you think that hasn't happened?'

Staff shrugged and slid his empty hand from his pocket. 'Don't know. Sounds pretty unlikely in the first place. Would have been nice, though.'

'Yes.' Staff had moved from confused to complacent once more. Kane took a deep breath. He didn't want to hurt him. He had given up that kind of life when he met Bella. 'Instead we have a society that's split in two: those that are afraid, and those that are angry. The afraid have fled, or locked their doors and stayed, trembling, under their blankets. The angry have taken the streets, and destroyed anything of beauty they could find.'

'They haven't destroyed this.' Staff tapped the case he carried.

'No. Can I ask where you got it? You're not my original contact, are you? '

'A friend of a friend.' He shrugged. 'He didn't think you'd show. Why spend your money on art when the world's about to change?'

'Let's just say money is less of a priority to me.'

Staff smiled without humour. 'That's a nice position to be in. So what are your priorities? Fun times? The good of humanity? '

'Old fashioned love, I'm afraid.' This was not something Kane would ever have chosen to discuss; he was surprised at himself. But here they were, on top of the world. They would never meet again. This time tomorrow they might not even be alive. What harm could a little honesty do? 'I've got someone I care about. It's a gift for her, to make up for... mistakes I made in the past. Whatever makes her happy.'

Staff lifted the case. 'And this will make her happy? She's got expensive tastes.'

'Yes,' Kane agreed. 'She's got class. Not beautiful, but very classy. Beauty – cover girl beauty, I mean – never mattered anyway.'

'Maybe it mattered to her.'

'You're right.' Kane evaluated his companion as the capsule shuddered through the docking platform and then started a slow ascent once more. 'I could easily have made her beautiful, but she says a plastic surgeon can't give her what fate decided she shouldn't have.' He smiled at the memory.

'So what did you do, to earn all this money? Who were you?'

'Someone who created misery,' Kane said softly, crossing his legs and pulling at the creases in his trousers. They had been made by a tailor in Hong Kong; he wondered where that small, precise man with such skill was right now. Maybe locked in his shop, or making a last suit for himself.

'An arms dealer? A politician?'

'I edited a newspaper. One of the newspapers that ran the story that triggered all this. We didn't know what they wanted, the aliens, but we found some crackpots who were willing to predict the worst and ran the story anyway.'

Staff laughed. 'You think you caused the end of the world? That's what I call an ego. The moment those lights appeared, it was going to happen. Besides, who's to say they're not going to kill us all? Maybe they're the judge and executioner of the universe. God knows we've been asking for it for long enough.'

'You think so?' And Kane could see he meant it. He reminded him of himself, when he was young and thought himself invincible. 'So what did you do? Before?'

'Worked in a bar. Got the job straight from my GCSEs. My friends used to come there and I'd give them cheap drinks, you know how it is. They didn't have jobs. They were into things, dodgy stuff. I'd listen to them doing their deals, but I didn't want to be like them, nicking mobiles, selling weed.

'Last week, and the lights came, and the papers – your paper – said it was the end of the world, and a few people believed them, and those few were so scared, so sure. The lights didn't move, they didn't change, and soon everyone else started to crack, and they all believed it was the end. I didn't know what to do, so I carried on going to work as usual, hoping my friends would turn up and take me with them, wherever they were going. I watched people run past the window, struggle with suitcases to make it to the tube, crash their cars into each other, scream, cry: it was crazy, crazy.

'Then it went quiet. My friends never came. They never came.' Staff swallowed, his attention fixed on the sky through the clear curved plastic of the capsule. Kane watched the jerk of his prominent Adam's apple. 'This man came in to the bar,' he said. 'He was carrying this case. Not much older than me, but strong, big shoulders, knew how to handle himself. He asked for a drink. Well, he asked for as much drink as he could handle. I would have given it to him for the company, but he was determined to pay. Said he'd never taken something for nothing in his life, and wasn't about to start now. So he told me about you, and the deal you'd set up before the lights came. He thought you wouldn't show, but said if you did, you'd give me something in return for that.' He passed the case to Kane, who put it on the floor, against his knee. 'Something worth more than money. Something that would change my life forever. So here I am.'

Kane smiled. 'Waiting for your reward. Very patiently, I might add.'

'I can be patient.'

The capsule was at the zenith of its orbit once more; they were as close to the lights as it was possible to get. Beneath them, on the other side of the river, smoke was thick, creeping over Whitehall. Something was on fire. Kane realised he was expecting to hear fire engines, maybe screaming. He tried to stop himself from straining to catch sounds that wouldn't come.

'Last week, if I had come here and looked down over London, I would have felt nothing,' he mused. 'When I was in the Army, before I became a journalist, I saw the worst side of humanity. Wars, famines, murders, rapes, despots – I saw it all, and decided that we're a fucked-up bunch. Pretty much all of us. So I decided not to give to charity. Not to watch appeals on television with huge-eyed orphans or starving children. They would only grow up to be scum like the rest of us, anyway.'

Staff sat on the opposite bench and leaned forward, his hands on his knees. 'At least you were honest.'

'I've always been honest. I've prided myself on that. If we'd met here to do our deal last week, I would have told you without any qualms that all the people who were walking the streets down there, considering takeaway for dinner or rushing for the start of the latest Hollywood bullshit, were no better than ants: not looking at each other, hardly aware of each other's presence, feeling love and hate for reasons they didn't understand.

'I had no respect for the people who bought my paper and bought into my headlines. They had their eyes closed, and I thought they'd never open them and see the truth.'

'You were right,' Staff said, and Kane had to stop himself from shouting.

'No! Don't believe that. Not now.'

'I see that everyone's run away. To look after themselves. Number one, that's all that matters. We're worse than insects – at least insects would fight to defend their kind.'

'We still might. Everything's changed,' Kane said, and he realised that was true. He had changed too. 'The rules are being rewritten, I promise you. And the fact that there's a man out there who decided he had no use for what I was going to give him is proof of that.'

Staff shook his head. The capsule was approaching the docking platform; they had come down from the clouds. 'No reward could make that much difference now anyway.'

'Here it is,' he said. 'You can make up your own mind.' He reached into his raincoat pocket and pulled out a flat box made of brushed metal, no bigger than his hand. It felt warm to his touch. He leaned forward and held it out to Staff.

'What is it?'

'A weapon.'

Staff's hand stopped, his fingertips just touching the box. He met Kane's eyes. 'What kind of weapon?'

'Biological. There's a vial attached to a dispersal device. You can look. It's safe in the box.'

Kane watched Staff's face as his fascination overcame his fear. He took the case and flipped open the catch. Kane looked away, up to the lights in the sky; he didn't need to see the neat plastic pistol nestling in the blue velvet lining. He had stared at it, considering his decision to trade it, for the past week.

'How does it work?' Staff whispered.

'Simple, I'm told. Just like a gun: you pull the trigger. Fire it into the sky and it'll blanket a square mile. The airborne virus will be inhaled and you'll have an infectious population walking about for three days before symptoms start to show. Death will follow in another seven to ten days. This could destroy a city. Or potentially go global. Of course, once it's released, there's no controlling it, is there? Totally random. A weapon of desperation.'

When Kane looked down, Staff had closed the box and placed it on his knees. His hands were in his hair; they were trembling. 'Why? Why did the man in the bar – why did he want this?'

Kane shrugged. 'I didn't ask.'

'You didn't ask? But what if he wanted to – he must be some sort of terrorist -'

'He wanted something badly, obviously. Maybe something political, maybe not. I didn't want to know.' He saw the incredulity in Staff's face. 'I told you. My wife was dead. I had only one thing that interested me, and I would do anything to get it. I knew the right sort of people to get hold of the item; I contacted them, and didn't think past that.'

'You'd give this weapon away for a painting?'

'For what the painting could give me, yes.'

'You traded multiple deaths to get laid.'

Kane shook his head. 'I know it seems bad. Evil. But it's not the worst thing I've ever done, believe me.'

Staff stood up and put the case, softly, on the bench. 'I don't believe you.'

'Let me tell you what the worst thing I ever did is. I was seven. I gave my sister chicken pox.'

'I don't find this funny.'

'Well, it's true. I walked into her room and breathed on her in her sleep. I wanted to scratch so badly, and I thought spreading the pain around would make it better.' He pictured himself, tiptoeing into the dark pink sanctum, past the small chair occupied by a close pack of cuddly toys, over the red skirt and white tights strewn on the floor, to stand by his sister and lower his head to hers. 'It was the one truly selfish thing I did. No redeeming side to it. I was thinking only of myself.'

Staff picked up the box from the bench. 'So giving me this – is an act of altruism, is it?'

'A deal is a deal,' Kane said, and he meant it. He had made his peace with it.

The capsule was only a foot from the ground. Staff swung back the door, hopped out and jogged to the control booth. A moment later, the capsule came to a halt on the platform and the trip was over. Kane picked up the rectangular case by its frayed strap and stepped down.

Staff crossed to him and held out the box. 'What shall I do with this?' he said.

Kane didn't take it. 'That's your decision.'

'You could at least throw out some ideas,' Staff said, and he had to laugh.

'All right… go home and put it under your pillow, keep it secret, and use the sense of power it gives you to infuse your daily life. Or maybe take it round the corner and use it right now; what difference would it make? The world's screwed anyway. But if I were you…'

'If you were me?'

'I'd wait. See what happens. Maybe the aliens will come down here tomorrow and start to round us up for orderly disposal, and then you'll have an option. Who knows what that stuff will do to them?'

'Who knows,' Staff echoed. He sucked in his cheeks and tilted his head to one side. 'Right then.'

'Right.'

'Enjoy your painting. I hope it's worth what you paid for it.'

'I hope so to.' Kane watched the young man walk away along the riverside, his pace fast, his head high.

*

The broken streetlight blinked on.

The man stood in the doorway of the hotel. With one hand he tapped the bottom of the large rectangular case he carried against the shiny toecaps of his shoes; with the other hand he flipped open his mobile phone and pressed a button.

'Rosebud,' he said. 'I've got it. Come down.'

The streetlight blinked off.

Close by, maybe a street away, there were loud calls, laughter, shouting; a group of young men, maybe a mob. Alcohol and mania were audible in their voices. The sound intensified, then began to ebb away.

A door squeaked open. 'I'm here,' a woman whispered. 'Give it to me.'

There was a rustle, then a sigh. 'Is it okay?' the man said.

The streetlight blinked on.

The woman was past middle age, tall and carrying weight on her hips. She was dressed in grey trousers and a waisted leather jacket. Her bouffant hair was brittle blonde, and her face was thick with make-up that did not disguise the sprinkle of deep pockmarks on her cheeks and chin.

She held up a canvas. Upon it was painted, in swirls of dark green and yellowing white, a vase filled with open, blousy roses. The oil was dense and the brushmarks bold. In the bottom right hand corner there wre the black twirls of a famous signature: Vincent.

'It's perfect,' the woman said. She knelt down and put the painting back in its case.

The light blinked off.

'We should go,' the man said. 'The streets aren't safe.'

'Is anywhere?'

There was a silence.

'You will come with me now, won't you?' the man said. It was a weary voice, but behind it, hidden in the question, was the insecurity of a little boy who had done wrong and was afraid of punishment. 'You do forgive me now, Rosebud?'

'I forgive you. And I'll come with you. Wherever you think we should go.'

There were footsteps: fast, neat footsteps, moving away, diminishing, until they could no longer be heard. The streetlight stayed off. It had given up its struggle.

Slowly, gradually, the lights in the sky grew brighter.

Happiness Comes With a Paper Umbrella and a Measure of Grenadine

Here you go, sir. One Happiness, the cocktail of cocktails, served with a twist.

What's that? A pretty face? It's kind of you to say, but I think you'll find it's the dim lighting and the glamour of my occupation evoking that illusion. Plus the tiny uniform and the ridiculously high heels. It's all part and parcel of the role, one might say.

Do you mind if I rest my tray on your table for a moment? I've got a jug of Happiness for table fifteen, and it's tiring on the arms.

Not that I'm complaining. Each and every one of these cocktails sold gives me a personal sense of satisfaction. Would you like to know why?

Before this evening, before I met you, and back before I began working as a waitress in a cocktail bar, I was that most downtrodden of creatures, a Clerical Worker. I used to process information for life assurance applications, and that gave me access to medical records. I could see every ailment people had visited their GP about, and apart from the usual high points involving sexually transmitted diseases and injuries involving vibrators or vacuum cleaners, it made for boring reading. Most people are a lot less unique in the medical department than they would like to think.

The two ailments I saw most often were, without a doubt, back pain and depression. One in three people, I would say, suffered from one or the other, and one in five from both. I used to wonder if one illness caused the other. Did depressed people stoop more? Or did having a bad back make a person really glum? How was it possible that so many people could be suffering from the same ailments? At that time, I didn't suffer from either.

How about you? You look like the afflicted type to me. Pain in the lumbar region? Worries about the world? Believe me, nowadays, I know where you're coming from.

But I was a different person back then, in lots of ways. I was keen to succeed in the field of clerical work, and in order to do that I had to impress one person in particular: Kirstie Kay.

Kirstie Kay was the head of my department, and she was everything I wanted to be. Kirstie wore expensive black skirts that made my grey trousers look like bespeckled victims of a lint attack. Kirstie smelled of perfume that could never have been bought from the old lady who came to my doorstep regularly, pronouncing her Ding Dong catchphrase in a high wheeze. Kirstie had her hair cut more regularly than just at Christmas and Easter so her mother didn't complain about her fringe getting in her eyes. Kirstie commanded respect.

What's that? You want another cocktail? You drank that one a little too fast, huh? I'd be careful, if I were you. These ones have a kick. But, since you're doing such a good job of listening, why don't you top yourself up from the jug on my tray? Help yourself – just don't say I didn't warn you.

Where was I? Oh yes. Respect. I respected Kirstie. I wanted to be just like her, but in order to climb the greasy pole of management I needed to find a way to gain her attention, a way to make me worthy of her notice.

It was only after watching the way she shrugged off all responsibility for any actual work by alternately charming and bullying her employees in group weekly update meetings that a solution came to me. And do you know what that solution was?

113

Manipulation.

I know what you're thinking. You're thinking that hard work and puckering to the boss's posterior might have offered a more traditional answer, but hear me out.

It was all very well to be mindlessly keying in all day, as requested, but to rise above the rabble I had to prove I could get results by analysing to my advantage. After all, that was the point of having a manager, wasn't it? To get results. And I intended to get the kind of results that would reveal my intelligence and capability to the world.

I read up on spreadsheets and put together a database of gargantuan proportions; one which allowed me to input the age, postcode, occupation, pastimes, and alcohol and cigarette consumption levels of every person who disclosed both back pain and depression on their applications. I was determined to find some common linkage. When I tracked it down, I was going to present it to Kirstie Kay, proving that I was capable of thinking outside the box and inside the management mindset.

It took three months of collation before results started to emerge, and another three months before I was sure of what I was seeing. During that time I worked overtime every day, even weekends, in the excitement of surreptitiously establishing a pattern, and had given myself chronic eyestrain and a permanent pain between my shoulder blades from all that screen staring and keyboard tapping, but those were minor considerations in the face of the information my project was providing. I had uncovered something astounding, and it was with trembling hands that I e-mailed Kirstie Kay and arranged a one-to-one meeting with her for the following Monday morning. I spent an anxious weekend checking my results again and again; I don't think I slept at all.

Another cocktail? Mind you, I really don't think you should. I wouldn't advise anyone to consume three in a row. You're making fast work of that jug. I suppose I should go and get a refill for table fifteen, but they look pretty out of it. They won't notice if they wait for a little longer.

To continue – we sat down in her office at 10:45am, facing each other over her walnut desk, Kirstie sitting with legs crossed in her leather armchair, me sitting with arms crossed in a standard plastic chair.

'Well, Leanne, you've intrigued me,' she said. Leanne isn't my name, but I was much too in awe of her to correct her. 'What did you want to chat about?'

I launched into my set speech, trying not to be distracted as she tapped the fingers of her left hand against the dial of the watch on her right wrist.

'What, Kirstie, in your opinion, would be the two illnesses we see disclosed on life assurance applications more often than any others?'

She leaned back in her chair. 'Well, Leanne, I wouldn't know. I could phone up our Statistical Analysis Department and get an answer for you.'

It came as a blow to learn of the existence of a Statistical Analysis Department, but I had put in too much work to refuse at the first fence.

'Actually, I already know the answer. It's back pain and depression. I calculated it myself – in my own spare time,' I added, when she raised one fine line of an eyebrow. 'And I also looked into what kind of people suffer from those illnesses, particularly when they occur together.'

For the first time since we had started working together five years ago, she looked at me with interest. 'Oh yes?'

'And I found out that, according to a database I've been keeping…'

'Yes?'

'…there is a ninety-three per cent correlation between back pain and depression appearing in tandem on the medical disclosures of life assurance applications…'

Her fingers had stopped tapping on her watch. They were curled into her palms, the knuckles white, and her elbows were on her desk as she leaned towards me. 'Yes?'

'...submitted by those people who list their occupation as Clerical Worker.'

There was a silence. It stretched on as she stared at me. I shuffled my papers in embarrassment, and the rustle seemed to prompt her back into action. She jumped up from her leather armchair and spoke, without her usual eloquence, I have to say.

'Sit there,' she said. 'Don't move.'

Then she walked out of the office.

I harboured a number of fantasies in the forty-five minute wait that ensued. I imagined she would return with the Managing Director, a five feet one inch tall Australian tycoon, who would listen to my revelation and immediately to promote me to head of the Statistical Analysis Department. At the half hour point I wondered if she would return with a media crew from the local television network, and urge me to divulge to them what I had just told her. At around the fortieth minute I began to feel concerned that she wasn't coming back at all.

So it was rather a disappointment when she returned with only a piece of paper, and her usual expression of smooth superiority firmly back in place.

She started talking as she walked around her desk to the window, and she looked alternately from the view of Reading high rises to a spot between my eyebrows.

'I've checked with the manager of our legal department and he asked me to remind you that, under section 17e of your contract, you are not at liberty to divulge any information pertaining to or, indeed, extrapolated from the processing of company application forms, okay Leanne?'

I didn't even remember seeing a contract, let alone section 17e. Then a vague memory of Induction Day came back to me – something had been whisked under my nose, something with thirty plus pages of very small print I had duly signed along with the other new starters. I suppose that must have been the arrival of the shackles, to which she was now drawing attention for the first time.

'Nobody needs to know,' she said, pronouncing each word very slowly.

'But we have to make the public aware about the dangers of clerical work…'

'No, we don't.'

'But they need to be told…'

'No, they don't.'

And then it dawned on me.

The company already knew.

They knew what illnesses were waiting to befall nearly all their ground level employees.

That explained why the managers got better chair with ergonomic support built in, and spent more time walking around than staring at the screen. That explained the long tea breaks and active holidays. These weren't just perks. They were measures designed to take care of the employees the company actually cared about.

Kirstie must have seen the moment of revelation on my face. 'If you tell a soul, they'll get you,' she said, not unkindly, I thought. 'And I'm not talking about a lawsuit. I'm talking about revenge. There's a lot of money at stake.'

I sat still in the chair and thought about it.

'That's right,' she said. 'Keep quiet. Go back to your desk, delete that database, and get on with your job.'

I got up. I went back to my desk and picked up the top application form on the pile, and processed it. And after that one I did another, and another, and it transpired that I worked solidly, without speaking one word to Kirstie Kay or anybody else for that matter, for the rest of the month.

It was about that time that I was diagnosed with serious depression.

The doctor prescribed Prozac. It's amazing stuff, giving a spreading sense of relaxation. And the best thing is, it's easy to get more, to get a huge supply by registering at different practices around the city. Nobody ever checks.

The second best thing is that it can be taken in conjunction with a high dosage of codeine – the codeine keeps the pain from my back and neck problems at bay. Those started when I worked all those overtime hours, hunched over the computer screen.

Anyway, at the end of that month the company announced a downsizing initiative, and I was one of the first to go, rewarded with a lump sum for not making a fuss. I put that money towards my new hobby: drinking. It seemed as good a pastime as any, and fulfilled all the criteria which a hobby should – it made the time pass more quickly and gave me a warm glow inside. I had a beer phase, followed by a wine phase, and then I moved into cocktails.

I've tried just about every combination known to man, from the standard gin base – Rickey, Gimlet, Honolulu Shooter – through the vodka based drinks – Moscow Mule, Corniche, Screw-Up – and even the most obscure cocktails – Hammer Horror, Munchausen, Cute Fat Bastard In The Sack – and all of them tasted pretty great to me. There's something about those little paper umbrellas and precise wedges of exotic fruits that make me feel wonderful, particularly when combined with the pills.

I saw the advertisement for a waitress at this place about two months ago, and I knew I could do a good job of it. I know by heart the recipe of any drink you can name; that's something the boss found out when he interviewed me. He gave me the uniform right after that first meeting, and I was working the next day.

I was hardly expecting – and you'll love the irony of this – one of my very first clients to be Kirstie Kay.

She was slumped, alone, at one of the tables – in fact it might have been this very table – and she beckoned me over to order a clutch of Zombies without once looking at me.

Her choice of tipple told me all I needed to know. Zombies have a reputation in the cocktail community. They do the job quickly and very thoroughly. She was out to get hammered.

I drank in her radically altered appearance as I returned, weaving my way through the tables, with her order. The black skirts had been replaced with mustard yellow leggings that showed off rather less than taut skin tone around her thighs. The designer jacket had been replaced with a black tee shirt that was emblazoned with a hot pink paint stain over her right breast.

118

'Been decorating?' I asked her as I placed down her order.

She took a mouthful of the first Zombie before replying, 'Mmm,' she said, which I took as an affirmative.

'New house?' I asked.

'Flat,' she said, and downed her first drink. Then she looked up at me.

It took a moment for recognition to sink in. She squinted, and then laughed. 'Leanne,' she said. She still had my name wrong, but this time round I didn't have the heart to correct her. 'Leanne. They downsized me. To a worker. To a sodding Clerical Worker.'

I had to ask. 'Back pain?'

She winced and laid one trembling hand on her coccyx.

'Depression?'

She nodded and burst into tears.

'You know what really gets me?' she said through the sobs. 'I've had to sell my house and get a crummy flat just round the corner from this dump, and I've had to apply for a new mortgage to do it. Do you know what the bank said? They said I had to get life assurance to cover the mortgage. Do you know what the life assurance company – my employer – said? They said I'd have to pay triple premium because of my back pain and depression. The back pain and depression that they sodding caused!'

I shrugged as I handed her a paper napkin. I have to admit I didn't feel much sympathy for her. 'Bad deal, Kirstie.'

'You still don't get it, do you? It's no bad deal. It's planned. It's all been planned.' She downed the second Zombie in one swift movement. 'Why do you think the insurance sector is the biggest grossing business in the UK? Why do you think they employ so many clerical workers who they encourage to sit on their arses and do very little work all day? Why have we become a nation of Administrators?'

As I walked away from her table, leaving her to a lifetime of crippling mortgage repayments and medication, it occurred to me that she was absolutely right. This was no series of coincidences.

We are a nation plagued with sad faces and bad backs for a reason. The terrible seating position and the grindingly boring jobs ensure that our money will be returned, in large, unavoidable amounts, to the people who employ us in the first place.

And from that knowledge, the cocktail known as Happiness was born.

No-one but me knows what goes into my cocktail. I made the first batch that very evening, and gave one to the boss to taste, and he's been selling them like crazy ever since. It's going to make my fortune. I've already had an offer to go nationwide through a distribution company based in Swindon.

You really want to know what goes in them, huh? Well… will you promise not to tell anybody? You will? Cross your main aortic valve?

Happiness consists of the following ingredients: three measures of gin, one measure of cherry liqueur, one egg white, one measure of grenadine, half a measure of whipped cream, one crushed up codeine tablet to be dissolved in the gin, one crushed up Prozac tablet to be applied around the rim of the glass, one optional squeeze of lemon, one umbrella and three maraschino cherries to garnish.

Of course, I wouldn't have told you if I wasn't absolutely sure that you'll keep my secret. Look at you. Such a kind face, as you sleep like a baby, slumped over the table top. I warned you not to drink so much, but would you listen to a mere waitress at a cocktail bar?

You're not the first OD we've had here, and you won't be the last. The ambulance will get here shortly, I'll tell them you've drunk far too much, you'll get your stomach pumped, and you'll probably wake up with one hell of a hangover and no memory of this conversation. That's a shame, because I like you. I really do.

STRANDS

The ability to be honest had left her a while ago, and so her calm temperament had been buried under the frustrations she was no longer able to admit to. Previously she had felt justified in letting everyone know just how unfulfilled she was, but now she had everything she had pursued: a husband, a baby, a career of sorts. To tell the truth and say none of these things were what she'd thought they would be seemed shameful, although she supposed lots of people felt that way. It was only that she had never considered herself to be one of those people – the type who got what they claimed they wanted and moaned about it afterwards.

Still, it grew, this bud of dissatisfaction, until she could feel it tapping its sturdy little shoots against her internal walls, and she knew it was only a matter of days before it found a way through her defences.

*

As it turned out, it wasn't a matter of days. It was a matter of years.

Poppy was about to start school. Her uniform had been bought, name tags sewn into the jumpers and the skirts, and they were counting down on the calendar to the day with the big red cross. The sense of expectation ruined everything Faye tried to do. Her yoga was fast and jerky, and her hand-made cards had jagged edges and a rushed look to them that she couldn't correct.

Matt came home late from work with a friend in tow, and although that was unusual, she was too tetchy to let new company please her. For a start, she was already in her dressing gown. She had bathed with Poppy before putting her to bed and reading her a Just So story – doing all the things that were expected of her so that nobody could suspect that she didn't actually enjoy spending time with her daughter.

She was busy submerging her usual attack of guilt for the evening in a soap opera when she heard the back door open and close, then voices, and laughter.

'Faye? Is there any red wine?'

'Just what's in the rack,' she called, then got up from the sofa and wandered into the kitchen with half a mind to be unpleasant.

The man stood with his back to the sink, his hands stretched out along the counter. He looked old and tired. He looked up at her with evident surprise. 'Hello,' he said.

Matt straightened from the wine rack with the neck of a bottle of Merlot in his hand. He had already removed his tie and undone the top button of his shirt; his jacket hung over the back of the metallic counter stool. He kept fit during his lunch hours, and every day looked more as if he belonged in a glamorous life that was taking place somewhere else. 'Phillip, this is my wife, Faye.'

'Hello,' Phillip said again, and she revised her first impression of him. He wasn't old, although he was undoubtedly older than her. His greying hair was cut close to his head, revealing high temples and large ears, and although there were long, sloping lines on his face his eyes and mouth were generous and energetic – the features of a boy who had not yet been taught to keep his emotions from his face.

Faye tightened the belt of her dressing gown over the persistent bulge of her womb. It seemed obvious to her by the way he held his head that he liked her.

'I'll go and get changed,' she said. 'Have you eaten?'

'Ate out,' said Matt. 'I meant to phone but the battery ran out on the mobile again. Didn't I ask you to remind me to charge it?'

That was Matt in a nutshell. He could handle the liquidation of huge companies, could lay off thousands of people at the behest of the accountancy firm he worked for without blinking, but was unable to realise that the objects he relied upon every day just needed a small amount of maintenance. His pen ran out, or his car missed a service, and then invariably he tried to put the blame on Faye, as if it was the duty of a wife to maintain his life for him while he worked on more important things.

'Please don't get dressed on my account,' said Phillip, and his voice had a tone of humour in it that made her smile back at him despite her resolution to be annoyed.

'All right,' she said. 'I won't.' It came out, in the strangest way, like a challenge. Matt was battling with the corkscrew, and didn't seem to notice.

'Grab the good glasses and take them through to the lounge, will you? We're celebrating. Closed an account at work.'

'Well done.'

She turned her back on them and walked self-consciously through the hall to the dining room, where she took three of the blue Murano glasses from display shelves. She cleaned off the dust on the hem of her dressing gown and walked back to the lounge with her mind on how she must look to Phillip – like a tame housewife? Or maybe, hopefully, a glamorous figure with her hair up from the nape of her neck and her silk dressing-gown sweeping the floor? She decided to believe he thought her beautiful. Then she could believe it herself, and act like a different woman because of it. A little pretence would be very welcome.

Phillip had taken the armchair by the recessed fire, and Matt was lying back on the sofa. She handed out the glasses and sat on the floor by Matt's legs, acutely aware of her bare feet, the soles facing Phillip as she stretched out her own legs and tucked her dressing gown under her knees.

Matt leaned over to Phillip and poured him a glass first, then Faye, then himself. The first sips passed in silence, as if they were connoisseurs rather than just ordinary people searching for something to say.

'Faye, how was your day today?' said Phillip.

'Fine,' she said, shocking into giving a boring answer.

'Not long until Poppy starts school now,' said Matt, in a hearty tone. 'Faye's dreading it.'

'Actually,' she said, 'I'm quite looking forward to having some more time for myself.'

'She'll be miserable at first. Still, she's got a little business, making greeting cards. It's going quite well, keeps her occupied.'

123

'Yes,' said Faye. 'Are you married, Phillip?'

'I have been. Three times.' He held his wine glass very lightly, his fingers moving up and down the long stem.

'Wow.'

'Yes,' he said, as if it was a puzzle to be solved, so she dared to ask about it.

'What went wrong?'

'Absolutely nothing.' Phillip wrinkled his nose at her, and she saw the lines around his mouth intensify. Exactly how old was he? 'I suppose I don't believe anything is forever.'

'I keep telling Phillip he should have kids,' said Matt. 'Kids make you appreciate just what forever means.'

'That's true,' she said.

'You're not committed to anything unless you choose to be,' Phillip replied, in a friendly tone, but she noticed how upright he sat, how he hadn't removed his jacket or loosened his tie. He hadn't fallen for the idea that he could relax in her presence because she was a wife. She was surprised to discover she liked him at least as much as he liked her. She wanted him to stay longer.

'You're sure I can't get you something to eat?'

'No, no,' he said. 'I should get going.'

'You've only just got here!' said Matt, as she knew he would. He always tried to persuade guests to stay. 'C'mon, let's finish the red, and I'll open a bottle of something special.' That was his code for cognac, and that meant hangovers tomorrow and the smell pervading the house, her breath. But it also meant Phillip would have to take the spare bed, and she would make him breakfast in the morning. A little piece of him, left behind in the house, on the sheets, in the leftover crumbs on the fine china.

'Maybe another time,' he said.

From the top of the stairs came a trembling voice. 'Daddy?'

Faye felt such guilty relief that Poppy had called for Matt, not her. It was a gift – to be alone with an interesting man, to stay free of motherhood for a few moments longer. She leaned forwards so Matt could stand up, and his abrupt movements were filled with self-importance. He adored this part of parenthood – to be needed. 'That's my cue.'

'She probably just wants a kiss and a cuddle,' Faye said.

'That's my specialty.' He went out into the hall, and she heard him take the stairs at a faster pace. Then he spoke to Poppy in that special way he had. She could picture him picking her up, the way she nuzzled into the crook of his neck. It gave her a moment of pleasure to know she had created Poppy. It was a rare emotion, one she only experienced when she imagined father and daughter together.

If only she could have worked full-time. He was better at parenthood. It came naturally to him, and whenever she tried to explain how she didn't feel the same he talked of help or counselling, getting her fixed so things could go on as they were.

'Actually,' said Phillip, as he stood up, 'something did go wrong. With all three marriages. It takes both parties to believe in freedom to make that kind of arrangement work. Do you think a woman wants a man to be tied to her forever whether that brings happiness or torment?'

'Yes,' she said, liking the words he used, the big concepts of which he wasn't afraid. 'Or, at least, that men should be tied down and made as unhappy as possible as often as possible.'

She could tell she'd surprised him. 'Why is that?'

'How else can a woman make a man appreciate what motherhood is like?'

Straight away, she regretted saying it. The wall had finally been breached, and here, in front of this stranger. There was nothing that could be said to cover it. She didn't know him well enough to turn it into a joke – *you know me, my funny sense of humour*....

He licked his bottom lip. 'Not everybody has to be...'

'What?'

'You don't have to be here.'

'Is that your philosophy? Forgive me for saying so, but I can see why your marriages didn't work.'

'How so?'

125

She got to her feet too, and realised how close that brought her to him. Still, she held her ground. 'Sometimes it seems that men never love the way women do.'

'Is that a good thing or a bad thing?'

She heard snatches of a lullaby, Matt's deep, happy voice. Then Phillip cleared his throat. 'I have a convertible. A BMW. It's a warm night.'

'Really?'

And he would go, and she would be left here worrying about what he thought of her, who he would tell about what she'd said. Would the words 'bad mother' come out of that generous mouth? At the office, the next day, would she be relegated to the status of anecdote? It took her by surprise, this fierce longing to change the path of their meeting, to not be dismissed, to make him feel something real.

'Come out for a drive,' he said.

She had been so busy packaging herself as an embarrassment that she didn't hear him at first.

'A drive,' he said again.

'When?'

'Now.'

'I should...'

'Now,' he said. 'Quick.' And he held out his hand with an urgency in his face, as if the worst thing in the world would be for her not to take it, his fear so plain that she thought it would hurt him to be refused, so she took it and they left the room, through the hall, the kitchen, out of the back door, past the swing set and the empty bird feeder, down the alley to where the bins huddled, and out to the driveway. There was his BMW, silver, the roof down, parked behind their Megane.

Phillip was right. It was a warm night.

He opened the passenger door for her and she got in, tucked her dressing gown over her legs. As he walked around the front to the driver's side she looked around the street, between the evenly spaced streetlights to the paths of her neighbours' houses, and the formality of those painted front doors, and the hedges that had been trimmed into squares and rectangles. When he started to reverse the car, the noise was so loud that she pictured everyone running to the windows to stare out.

Beside her, he handled the car as men do, like a master guiding a dog, and without asking he reclined her seat from a button next to the handbrake so she could see up to the sky. There was only the haze of the lights of the city. Her sense of home, the strands of her that reached back to Matt and Poppy, spilled out behind her like spider silk, loose, bending, not even close to being stretched thin.

'I know a place,' said Phillip. 'In the country. You'll be able to see the stars out there. It's where I go when I want to be able to think.'

'About what?' she said, surprised to find her voice sounded the same.

He shrugged. His profile was less friendly than the full view of his face. His nose was a long straight line, regal, reminding her of a Roman coin. For the first time she suspected he might be capable of cruelty. 'I like to think about the path ahead.'

'That sounds very calculating.'

'I like to have a plan.'

'But this couldn't be part of your plan,' she said, meaning herself, and he replied:

'No. This wasn't in the plan.'

'Sometimes,' she said, 'when I make my cards, I picture the person who'll receive them, and what they'll be doing. Wedding days, births, condolences. Will they all be feeling what they're meant to be feeling?'

'Does it matter what other people think?'

She didn't reply, although she thought that nothing else could matter, and was surprised to learn he thought differently.

'I've made a mistake,' she said, then, 'Take me back, please.'

But Phillip didn't turn the car around, and so she didn't ask again. The excitement and fear his lack of obedience gave her was welcome. It was as if she couldn't properly feel. She wondered when reality would kick in.

Matt would have come back downstairs by now. She pictured him hunting around the house, in the way he did when he played hide and seek with Poppy, bending low, looking under beds and in the airing cupboard, and a laugh spilled out of her. How cruel she was. How terrible, and free.

They hit the motorway, and the long untroubled lanes took her further away, the strands still strong, still spooling.

After a while the scenery began to change. The flat plains curved upwards into hills, then forests, the trees pressing close. The motorway became a dual carriageway, then dual carriageway, then single track, and the speed of the car lessened, lessened, until it felt as if they were moving no faster than she could wait. She was cold, now, in the convertible, but she didn't ask for the roof to be put back up. To do so would be to accept that something had changed and she was not in the car to see the stars any more.

'Nearly there,' Phillip said.

'Where?'

'The place I know.' The new edge of tension in his voice put her on alert. What did he think was going to happen? How ridiculous she was not to have really thought about the possibility that he just wanted sex. Not that she hadn't considered having sex with him, but if he thought that was the reason she had got into the car, how belittling that would be.

Had Matt given up by now? Gone to sleep, assuming she'd be back in the morning, and no words would need to be exchanged about this transgression? Or did he think she had been taken against her will, spirited away?

Sometimes Poppy had bad dreams, and needed to hear the song about the sleepy elephant. Faye wasn't sure if Matt knew the words. She could see Poppy quite clearly at that moment. In bed, in that ridiculous position she always managed to end up in, her head against the bed rail, her feet on the wall, her pyjama top crumpled up and her face a blank sheet of peace in the purple glow of her nightlight.

That was responsibility; that clear image of the child who doesn't realise what adults are capable of, and holds her mother to ransom with her innocence.

The desire to get home was suddenly strong. She fought it down.

Phillip drove into a town, through the silent main street, and Faye realised hours had passed. They turned left and began to climb, and then there was a view of the sea, black as tar. A right turn, and in front of her was a manor house, two porch lights revealing grey pillars and a closed front door between many windows. The car stopped and she got out, feeling the painful prickle of gravel on the soles of her bare feet. Phillip came to stand beside her. 'They know me,' he said. 'I'll get a room.'

She looked at him and he touched her neck with one finger. There was something proprietorial in the gesture that made her want to brush him away, turn to him, demand proper answers. She could have said *What exactly do you think of me? What is it that you think is happening here? Explain this connection in words of one syllable, taking no longer than thirty seconds, so I can get to the bottom of this.*

But she said nothing, and he went to the door and rang the bell, one of the old ones that he had to pull out from the wall. It made no sound that she could hear.

While his back was turned she tiptoed across the gravel, bare feet smarting, and took a set of semi-circular stone steps down into an overgrown garden that stretched over the hill, leading down to the sea. She walked on, the path changing to wood chippings, easier on the feet, and she brushed past tall, leafy plants that she didn't recognise. The sense of being watched grew with each footstep – watched by animals, birds, by the sea itself. Yet she did not feel separate from the ground she walked upon, or the leaves she ran her hands across. She could hear the sea now, shushing her, assimilating her. For the first time since the birth of Poppy she did not feel out of place, or wrong.

Further down, the path petered out in the face of a wall of dense bushes, and as she pressed into them their wetness soaked her dressing gown, and their branches snagged the material. She undid her belt, slipped off the gown, and carried on in her short nightdress, letting the night air steal all her warmth away, take her heat and her emotions for its own.

Behind her, a voice -

'Faye!'

She crouched on an instinct, then turned, moving her head until she had a view of the path back through the leaves. Phillip was there, at the bottom of the stone steps, his close-cropped hair silver in the moonlight. He stood still and tall, and it struck her how handsome she found him, but she did not move.

He waited, as if it was inevitable that she would come to him, and the more he waited the more she turned against him. A man was never going to provide an answer; men, with their lives laid out in straight lines, like motorways, each emotion taken at a time, never overlapping, all in perfect order – daughter, job, house, wife, and always one part, the deepest part, free and clear. Men came with a fast lane, just for themselves, no baggage allowed.

How had she fallen for it?

Phillip looked over his shoulder, then out to the sea. He said something she couldn't hear, then called again: 'Faye!' The garden trembled at his voice.

He walked away.

And then there was nobody left to escape. The strands of her life, spilling out from her in all directions, didn't tighten, didn't pull at her. They were slack, and somehow the garden had freed her of all emotion: guilt, fear, love, sucked down into the soil and locked away, deep in the earth, like a foretaste of death, so welcome.

Faye pulled her nightdress up over her head and threw it away. She walked further into the bushes, heading for the sea.

ACKNOWLEDGEMENTS

Galatea first published by *Whispers of Wickedness*, January 2005.

Witchcraft in the Harem first published by *Sein und Werden*, April 2006; subsequently podcasted by *The Drabblecast*.

Wingspan first published by *The Future Fire*, September 2009.

Babyhead podcasted by *The Drabblecast*; subsequently published by *Allegory*, Winter 2012.

1926 in Brazilian Football first published by *Word Riot*, May 2008.

Lego Land first published by *Scifantastic*, March 2006.

The Bengalo Boys first published by *Fear and Trembling*, June 2007.

Legs first published by *Unlikely Stories*, November 2003.

Flushed first published by *3:AM*, June 2009.

Songs for Dead Children first published in *The First Book of Classical Horror* (Megazanthus Press, 2012)

Penelope Napolitano and the Butterflies first published by *Strange Horizons*, December 2011.

Midnight Midnight first published by *Jupiter*, July 2012.

Caterpillar first published by *The Laura Hird Showcase*, May 2004.

For Rosebud first published by *Fusion Fragment*, July 2008.

Happiness Comes With a Paper Umbrella and a Measure of Grenadine first published by *pulp.net*, September 2004.

Strands first published by *Ink Filled Page*, Summer 2009.

Thanks to Adam Lowe, Leanne Haynes and everyone at Dog Horn Publishing. Also thanks to those who first published these stories, particularly everyone who was part of *Whispers of Wickedness*, Norm Sherman at *The Drabblecast*, Laura Hird, and Des Lewis.

Neil Ayres, John Griffiths, Francesca Kemp, UKAuthors, my MNW friends – thanks for continuing to support me and believe in me.

Motherhood dominates this collection. Thank you to Nick and Elsa for making me a mother, and also understanding me as a writer.

Out Now:
Women Writing the Weird
Edited by Deb Hoag

WEIRD

1.   Eldritch:suggestingtheoperationofsupernaturalinfluences; "an eldritch screech"; "the three weird sisters"; "stumps . . . had uncannyshapesasofmonstrouscreatures"—JohnGalsworthy;"an unearthlylight";"hecouldheartheunearthlyscreamofsomecurlew piercing the din" —Henry Kingsley

2.   Wyrd: fate personified; any one of the three Weird Sisters

3.   Strikingly odd or unusual; "some trick of the moonlight; some weird effect of shadow" —Bram Stoker

WEIRD FICTION

1.   Storiesthatdelight,surprise,thathangabouttheduskyedges of'mainstream'fictionwithcharacters,settings,plotsthatabandon thenormalandmundaneandexplorenewideas,themesandwaysof being. —Deb Hoag

RRP: £14.99 ($28.95).

featuring

Nancy A. Collins, Eugie Foster, Janice Lee, Rachel Kendall, Candy Caradoc, Mysty Unger, Roberta Lawson, Sara Genge, Gina Ranalli, Deb Hoag, C. M. Vernon, Aliette de Bodard, Caroline M. Yoachim, Flavia Testa, Aimee C. Amodio, Ann Hagman Cardinal, Rachel Turner, Wendy Jane Muzlanova, Katie Coyle, Helen Burke, Janis Butler Holm, J.S. Breukelaar, Carol Novack, Tantra Bensko, Nancy DiMauro, and Moira McPartlin.

Out Now:
Bite Me, Robot Boy
Edited by Adam Lowe

Bite Me, Robot Boy is a seminal new anthology of poetry and fiction that showcases what Dog Horn Publishing does best: writing that takes risks, crosses boundaries and challenges expectations. From Oz Hardwick's hard-hitting experimental poetry, to Robert Lamb's colourful pulpy science fiction, this is an anthology of incandescent writing from some of the world's best emerging talent.

Featuring
S.R. Dantzler, Oz Hardwick, Maximilian T. Hawker, Emma Hopkins, A.J. Kirby, Stephanie Elizabeth Knipe, Robert Lamb, Poppy Farr, Wendy Jane Muzlanova, Cris O'Connor, Mark Wagstaff, Fiona Ritchie Walker and KC Wilder.

Out Now:
Cabala
Edited by Adam Lowe

From gothic fairytale to humorous pop-culture satire, five of the North's top writers showcase the diversity of British talent that exists outside the country's capital and put their strange, funny, mythical landscapes firmly on the literary map.

Over the course of ten weeks, Adam Lowe worked with five budding writers as part of the Dog Horn Masterclass series. This anthology collects together the best work produced both as a result of the masterclasses and beyond.

Featuring
Jodie Daber, Richard Evans, Jacqueline Houghton, Rachel Kendall and A.J. Kirby

Out Now:
Nitrospective
Andrew Hook

Japanese school children grow giant frogs, a superhero grapples with her secret identity, onions foretell global disasters and an undercover agent is ambivalent as to which side he works for and why. Relationships form and crumble with the slightest of nudges. World catastrophe is imminent; alien invasion blase. These twenty slipstream stories from acclaimed author Andrew Hook examine identity and our fragile existence, skid skewed realities and scratch the surface of our world, revealing another—not altogether dissimilar—layer beneath.

Nitrospective is Andrew Hook's fourth collection of short fiction.

RRP: £12.99 ($22.95).

Acclaim for the Author

"Andrew Hook is a wonderfully original writer" —Graham Joyce

"His stories range from the darkly apocalyptic to the hopefully visionary, some brilliant and none less than satisfactory"
—The Harrow

"Refreshingly original, uncompromisingly provocative, and daringly intelligent" —The Future Fire

ND - #0515 - 270225 - C0 - 234/156/11 - PB - 9781907133404 - Gloss Lamination